Hey Angel

ISBN: 978-1-7636049-9-5

Year of First Publication, 2024
Second Edition: March, 2025
10 9 8 7 6 5 4 3 2

Edited by Hannah Razay
Edited by Oaklin Charlesworth

Cover Design & Art by Joan P. Mathew

Hey Angel

Christian Paul D'Alessi

CONTENTS

For me.

HERE WE GO LOOP DE LOOP

I wake up slowly. My vision's blurry. My eyes feel heavy and it hurts to move them. Gazing at a shadowy corner of a ceiling in a sterile room. It's night and eerily quiet, but I pick up on a familiar sound: a rhythmic beeping. The more attention I give it, the louder it sounds. I think I'm in a hospital. Panic surges in my chest and I realise it's the only feeling I have in my body. *Ah fuck, what's happened?* My mind races; I can't think straight, and somehow, my head feebly rolls itself to the right, where I briefly glimpse a patient monitor. *I am in a hospital—fuck!* A sudden involuntary spasm returns my gaze to the shadowy corner of the ceiling. The void is calling my name and everything fades and I have no will but to surrender to the darkness of sleep.

I wake up slowly. My vision's blurry. Gazing at a shadowy corner—*I remember.* I can't move. *That beeping sound—*panic surges—*fuck me, why does this keep happenin'?* I can't think straight. The patient monitor—I spasm. The void whispers from the shadowy corner of the ceiling, and everything fades again to darkness.

I wake up slowly. My vision's blurry—the corner ceiling. I've lost count of how many times this keeps happening...*That fuckin' beeping sound!* I still can't move. The panic overwhelms me every time, and it sends my mind racing...I'm frightened. The patient monitor... The corner ceiling... darkness.

I wake up again and again, over and over, to that same goddamn empty ceilin' and the beeping—fuck! I still can't fuckin' move! Am I dyin'? Is this death? What is this? Just stop...please stop. Why won't it just fuckin' stop!? My chest...just kill me already—god—fuck!

I wake up. *Okay, I get it now...I'm dead. Or is this limbo...hell's waitin' room, waitin' for judgment? The panic and the loopin' vision and my inability to move...maybe this is hell.* I can't think straight. I fade to black.

* * *

I wake up slowly. My vision's blurry. Gazing at a shadowy corner—*That beeping sound—I'm in a hospital! Car crash—I remember! A panic surges—Angel!...we were drivin'. Think straight. We were drivin', and we're... we, we couldn't believe it... no! Crashed and, and...the patient monitor—no!* A sudden involuntary spasm returns my gaze to the shadowy corner of the ceiling, and the void calls my name again, and everything fades, and I have no will but to surrender to the darkness of sleep.

* * *

I wake up slowly. My eyes hurt. My vision's blurry. Gazing at a shadowy corner of a ceiling in a sterile room. It's night and eerily quiet, but I pick up on a familiar sound—and I remember—I'm in a hospital, and I don't need to panic. Just need to remain calm. Try to remember how I got here. *I was drivin', and Angel was in the passenger seat, and we... won? Wait? No! We had an accident and, and...*and panic surges in my chest —I can't move my body—*fuck! Calm! Calm... My mind...my mind is calm...* I can think straight. *Angel and I were in a car crash; I'm alive in a hospital and...and she's...*I don't know. I'm suddenly overwhelmed by fear. I spasm, my gaze returns to the shadowy corner of the ceiling, and the void calls for me. Everything fades, and I can't resist it, again, to the darkness.

I wake up slowly. My eyes hurt and so does my body, but I still can't move. My vision's blurry, gazing at a shadowy corner of a ceiling in a sterile room. It's night and eerily quiet, and I ignore the rhythmic beeping. My mind is calm. I can think straight. *Me and Angel were in a car crash. I'm alive in a hospital and she is...she's alive. I need to get 'outta here. I need to get to Angel.* I look to my right, where I briefly glimpse a patient monitor. I try to focus and look past it. I see a window at the end of the room. The curtain is open, and I can see the night sky and the city skyline, lit up like a Christmas tree... there's no spasm. I return my gaze, and...a nurse? I see a nurse...*and she can see me!* We lock eyes. *Yes! Oh god, yes! I'm not dead.* She quickly dashes out of the room, calling for a doctor, and then I see that shadowy corner of the ceiling again, and everything fades, and I try to resist it, but...

I wake up slowly. My eyes don't hurt, and I can move them, gazing at a shadowy corner of a ceiling in a sterile room. It's night and eerily quiet, but I pick up on a familiar sound: a rhythmic beeping. I give it no attention. I remember the nurse. *I'm in a hospital.* I focus my attention on my body and try to move. I start with my right hand, feeling for something to touch, and I do; I can feel the bedsheets. I go for it and lift my arm to my face. *I can see my arm!* I pull the ventilator away from my face and attempt to sit up... I can sit up... Blood rushes to my head. I wait for it to pass. *Gotta take it slow. I can't let the dark sleep return.* I sit for a while and look around. I'm alone in an intensive care unit. The curtains are draped, but there's a gap, and I catch a glimpse of the moon. *How long have I been 'ere?* My body feels gross and moist with sweat. I take it easy, dragging the blankets away. *Thank Christ, I have my legs. I don't think I could handle seein' my legs amputated. Fuck me. They're so thin.*

A chill runs down my back, but it's welcomed. The taste in my mouth to the back of my tongue is coarse and vile. My gums throb, and my teeth ache. There's a needle in my arm with a tube connected that leads back to a machine; it must be feeding me. I pull it out, and an alarm goes off. The sound makes my eardrums pulse. A nurse enters the room and freezes, shocked by the sight of me. She rushes to my side, adamant that I lie down. I try to brush her away, but I'm too weak. She tells me to lie down, then presses a button on the wall.

I try to speak, but it hurts. My mouth moves, but nothing comes out. Another nurse enters, and this one dashes to my other side. The nurses are considerate but forceful as they lay me down. I don't fight them. I can't. They inform me I'll be okay and that they'll immediately have a doctor attend. They're still startled.

'Isn't this the patient police wanted to question?' One nurse asks the other.

The second nurse shrugs.

Police? *Shit.* I try to muster enough strength to speak again. *I need to get 'outta here—I need to get to where Angel is.*

But again, it hurts, and nothing comes out. The nurses' expressions turn to sorrow, and catching each other on it, they try to hide it. *They know somethin'...somethin' horrible has happened.* I'm lying down and see the corner ceiling; everything fades, and I fall asleep.

* * *

I wake up slowly. I remember moving. I remember the nurses. I sit up and look around the room. I'm alone...*but for how long?* I remove the ventilator from my face and take a deep breath. My arm has needles and tubes attached to it. I want to pull them out, but don't want to alarm anyone. Especially police. Piggies and I don't get along. I pull the blankets and sheets off my body—a welcomed chill down my back and neck. I try to move my feet and toes. There's a delay. If I keep pushing them, maybe my mind will catch up to my body...*or is my mind too far ahead? That makes no sense.* I lift my bony knees to my body and touch them with my hands, and it's alarming how withered they've become. I'm afraid to look at the rest of me. There's a door to a bathroom across the other side of the room. I slide my legs off the side of the bed and momentarily sit as my head spins like a kid taking his first drag of a cigarette. It must be the blood rushing throughout my body for the first time in a long time. The feeling passes. I slide off the side of the bed to my feet and hold tight to the bed frame.

I'm close enough now to switch off these machines attached to me from the wall. They don't set off alarms. I pull the needles and tubes out of me and slide my hand underneath my gown, feeling my chest for heart monitors, and unclip them. Hair on my chest—*that feels like me.* My mind and body are in sync—*I hope.* I take my first step in god knows how long. I feel goofy, like a newborn deer taking its first steps. The cold floor feels good and helps wake me from this fog. *Okay, step one is in the books; time for step two...*

I'm on the floor…and it hurts. I remain here until the pain passes and then attempt to stand again, but it's no good.

Half an hour has passed by. I'm gonna have to crawl to the door—see if any fuzz is outside. I worm my way over, and it hurts. Grasping at the door handle and using the window ledge alongside, I pull myself up. My upper body strength has withered. I manage enough height to peek through the blinds into the hallway. No one around. I collapse to the floor, out of breath. I look across the room towards the bathroom. What would typically be a matter of seconds feels like an eternity, but eventually, I reach the bathroom. The lights flicker on—*must've been triggered by motion sensors.* I crawl to the toilet and prop myself up on the seat. I rest here a while to gather myself and gaze toward the mirror above the basin a couple of meters away. *I know I'm gonna look like shit—Fuck it.* I pull myself together, stand, and approach the mirror one step at a time. My mind races a little, concerned about my appearance. *I don't know why now; I've never cared before.* I glance at the mirror, and my peripheral vision catches the initial glimpse before I fully turn to confront my reflection. I witness my jaw drop—my eyes well up with emotion. My legs go wobbly and I quickly clutch the basin, bracing myself against the overwhelming reality. I don't completely recognise myself. I have a partial bandage around the side of my head, and it extends around my neck, which could explain my difficulty speaking. My complexion is sickly. Dark circles cast shadows beneath my eyes, and I…I can't help but notice the fear in them. My facial hair has grown unchecked, and it's lengthy and uneven. I slowly remove my gown, uncovering my chest adorned with silvered hair and a pallid body that bears the marks of significant weight loss. I can see the outline of every muscle fibre and every rib… my cock is flaccid. I look weak and malnourished—*not since Afghan…*my legs go from under me again. I can't hold myself up on the basin any longer and stumble toward the toilet, taking a seat.

What the hell's goin' on? None of this adds up... Angel. I gotta find Angel. I push back the tears and swallow any sense of feeling sorry for myself. I've been here before. My body may have eroded, but my mind remains. *I sure as hell ain't gonna let Angel be faced with any of this shit. Gotta think—gotta think... The medical chart!*

I limp out of the bathroom, back into the intensive care room, and toward the end of the bed, where I pick up the medical chart hung to the back of the bed frame. Name... age...race...blah, blah, blah, where's the details? Motor vehicle accident...induced coma...major brain and body trauma... A spontaneous tremble courses through my body. I keep reading. Facial surgery...slipped into a prolonged coma...hydration and nutrition feeding tubes...recovery uncertain... I read the admission date, then skip ahead to the most recent notes—again, my legs go from under me, dropping the chart on the bed. I quickly brace myself and lean my weight over the bed—*fuck me.* I've been asleep for a year. I glance toward the window and try to focus my attention through the thin gap in the curtain. *Breathe...breathe.* I take a deep breath, straighten up and take the chart with me as I limp to the window. Sliding open the curtains, a sea of light glistens across the city skyline. It's beautiful... Then I see the Harbour Bridge and the Opera House and realise I'm back in Sydney. *Fuck. Could be worse; could be in Melbourne.* I continue reading the chart and all at once I wish I hadn't. I read Angel's name. A surge of dread engulfs me, followed by the brutal sensation of my heart being ripped from my chest and ruthlessly trampled upon. Then, I remember the chaotic loss of control, the lightning-fast trajectory of the car, and every jolt and collision as we smash through the highway barrier and plough through the underbrush and then... and then it all goes dark. I recall hearing a woman's voice, but it's not Angel's. I can't tell what's being said, but it makes me panic...

Angel's face suddenly flashes across my mind. She's stained with blood, dead—the chart slips from my grasp, and I collapse to the floor under the weight of emotion. It hurts so much to cry.

The floodgates open, and every long-buried hurt I kept chained up burns uncontrollably, pouring out of me, not just as tears but also as palpable energy from my chest and out through the crown of my head and the palms of my hands. In the throes, I make no sound. I can only wail agonisingly in silence.

Not again.
Why?
Why do you keep doin' this to me?
Why her?
She did nothin' to you!
I hate you.

I stare blankly at the shadowy corner of the ceiling with trails of dry tears crusted down my face. I'm exhausted. From outside, I hear the faint sound of an ambulance siren—an echoic memory overwhelms my senses—an argument; two voices. Suddenly, a flash of memory strikes me like a picture, a snap-shot of two kids; one has his hands on Angel...*what's happenin'...what's goin'...she's hurt, she needs... he's killin' her,* while the other, a woman, watches.

They could've helped her. Instead, they decided to kill—*I remember!* They chose to kill...*over some goddamn lottery.*

New feelings intensify in me; the flames of rage, a relentless hammering of anger, the fiery burn of hate, and a disconcerting clarity of violence transfix my mind. I lift myself off the floor, and I can stand firmly, as vengeance stokes strength from my feet to my head and in my clenched fists, I feel powerful. I look across the city skyline, clouds pass; a full-blood moon reveals itself—that means an eclipse is coming—a *symbol of change and transformation.* Angel taught me that. She was into that kinda thing, the moon and the stars.

Angel, my angel.

I need to get 'outta here. I need information. *Hopefully, that male nurse is still around—there's only one way to find out.* I move across the room towards the exit, gently twisting the door handle open just wide enough to poke my head out and peek around. A couple of nurses, both female, are talking shit at the nursing station, one wears a Santa cap, and the other wears reindeer antlers. Without making a sound, I bring myself back inside and close the door. *Scrubs all look the same to me, and those nurses will have to do—time to alarm some people.*

I look around the room for something sharp—something threatening. I don't want to hurt these girls, just scare them. There isn't much besides a pen attached to the chart. I walk over to the wall next to the bed and scope out all the buttons on it. None of them make sense to me. So I press them all, but nothing happens; no alarms go off. I plug the machines I removed earlier back in and start tapping buttons, making noises loud enough for them to hear. I hobble quickly behind the door and wait for a nurse to enter, and when one does, I'll keep her inside, threaten her and have her strip, exchanging my gown for her scrubs. I'll lock her in the bathroom too; that'll give me enough time to escape. *This'll work*—I hear footsteps but remain steadfast.

The footsteps pass. I wait a moment more. A year of unconscious sleeping may have affected my hearing. I wait a little longer, but still nothing. *Fuck it.* I bang on the door. *That oughta do it. …* But nothing—no one responds to the noisy machines or the banging on the door. *What the hell hospital is this?* I inch the door open and peek my head out again. It's bizarrely quiet, and the nurses are gone. I step out into the hallway and look around both ways. I clap, and the sound reverberates through the hallway…still nothing, no attention given—*I guess I shouldn't complain.* I leave the room and walk down the hallway past dark, quiet rooms and sleeping patients. The faint hum of machine monitors, ventilators and infusion pumps plays as background noise to my bare footsteps while I walk the lino flooring.

I come to an open ward that piques my interest: old folks sleeping. I tread warily inside and look for something to wear. A chair is at the end of one of the beds, and a three-quarter dark brown tweed coat hangs off the back. I run my hands over it, examining it. I like it. It's well-worn and smells like an old man: probably the old bloke in the bed asleep in front of me. He seems peaceful. Also on the chair is an old Ashwood leather travel bag. Inside is a pair of trousers and a couple of shirts. The old bloke hasn't updated his wardrobe since the 50s. *Beggars can't be choosers.* I put them on quickly. They're a loose fit, hanging off me like clothes pegged to a line.

Dressed, I touch the old bloke's foot, gesturing an apology and thanks, and at that moment, he opens his eyes and looks at me—*Jesus!* I pull my hand away, startled. But the old bloke doesn't seem panicked; his expression is calm, and his eyes expectant. Neither of us moves; we just look at each other. Then he smiles and closes his eyes, and his face softens with what appears to be his last breath. I've seen men die before, even one by my own doing, but none until now have ever made me feel safe. The monitor alongside the old bloke's bed alarms with a light above the entrance door of the ward, flashing red. I quickly grab his coat and flee.

At the end of the hallway, a nurse shouts for me to stop, but I dash to the elevators and press down. The floor indicators show this elevator is still several floors above—it's taking too long, so I hustle to my left down the stairs, gripping the side rail for support—I'm still moving a little gingerly. Again, the nurse shouts for me to stop. I keep moving.

Before exiting the foyer of the ground floor, I put on the old bloke's coat, pop the collar, and neaten my shaggy appearance, running my fingers through my hair. I straighten my posture and step out, casually walking with my head low.

Passing through the foyer, I realise I'm not wearing shoes. Not much I can do now but keep my cool—*almost out.* I casually stride down the exit steps and onto the street and around the corner, taking a right into a dark, lush park, and I'm out of sight.

It's a warm night, and it's welcomed as I stand under the blood moon surrounded by trees. My mind set on bad feelings, and for some unknown reason, I recall a quote.

"There is a red and angry world.
Red things happen there.
The world eats your wife.
Eats your friends.
Eats all the things that make you human.
And you become a monster."

I read that in a comic book, Swamp Thing... That's how I feel... that's what I am now, a monstrous swamp of things.

I got bad feelin's for those kids, gotta find 'em... But first, my Tweety Bird.

* * *

The throbbing pain in my left foot from having stubbed several toes on an uneven curb shortly after fleeing the hospital is a constant nuisance. I was bin-diving for half-eaten food trashed by a couple of kids outside a McDonald's. It was the first solid food I'd had in some time. Tasted great, but ten minutes later, I was vomiting in another bin.

I'm not confident with my perception of time. I've been walking the busy city streets barefoot for what feels like a couple of hours now. The smell and haze of bushfire smoke in the air tells me it's been a scorching summer and the pavements are only now starting to cool. The streets are excessively decorated with Christmas ornaments and lights, Christmas carols play from every shop, and storefront windows are filled with glittering merchandise to be sold. *Gotta keep movin'*.

* * *

I'm almost home. I pass an affluent-looking lady with a bleached white perm, wearing a puffy vest and walking a Pomeranian. *A puffy vest in this heat?* Seeing someone like her on this side of town doesn't make sense. She looks as if she's from Bellevue Hill. *The area couldn't have changed that much, could it?*

I turn a corner and look towards my apartment block. I'm the fifth window to the right on the sixth floor—lights are on. As the pain in my stubbed toes throbs, I stand on a concrete footpath, which is sticky with gunk and littered with filth and it occurs to me I'm not thinking straight. Of course, my apartment is no longer mine. I've been a vegetable for the past year. A police unit rolls up on my street—*shit!* I hide behind a telephone pole, wait till it passes, but it's not moving, just sitting idle—*shit!* I can't stay here, too suspicious looking… and my body feels as if it's gonna give out on me at any moment. I can't go knocking, not right now, not yet, and not in my condition and with police around. I'll have to get Tweety Bird some other time.

Some protestant church on the corner behind me is running a kitchen van outside for the homeless. Quietly, keeping my head low, I make my way over and join the line of society's forgotten withered dregs before grabbing one of those styrofoam mugs. *Hot soup will do me good.*

The police move on. The soup is healing, and as I glance over a pamphlet handed to me by the church pastor, I recognise I need help, and I hate needing help. But I'm unsure of a few things… *Candy.*

I see a sign, Hurstville. *Gotta find a train station.*

* * *

I hop a ticket barrier at Redfern station. An attendant sees me but he makes the right choice to back away as I stare ugly at him. When I step onto the escalator the sensation of vertigo kicks in, bringing nausea with it, so I keep my chin up, look ahead and try not to blink. It's worked in the past.

On the platform, several people look with disgust at me. Don't blame them. I move away, pop the collar on my coat and keep my head down while I survey the platform. I feel the rush of wind flowing as a train approaches. "MIND THE GAP" is stencilled in yellow along the platform's edge. The train pulls up, the double doors open, and I step on through, taking the closest seat to the exit.

I'd forgotten how unpleasant the bright fluorescent lights of a train carriage can be, tinged with a gross yellow. I try to rest anyway, hoping to regain some strength. *Damn, that soup was good.* The train pulls away, and I stare out the window. Everything becomes a blur, rushing quickly. It reminds me of the Coyote and Road Runner cartoons I watched as a kid.

I'm tired. I know I need to rest and sleep. But I'm afraid that if I do I won't wake up again. *Christ!* I didn't think to check what train line this was. I sit up and look around the carriage. I'm alone, with nobody to ask. Sinking back into the seat, not knowing where this train is heading, and like a jittery VHS tape, the vision of that kid's hand on Angel while the other watches loops on replay in my mind as the gentle motion and low, constant hum of the train carriage rocks me to sleep, fading fast. It feels right, and I want to surrender. *Who are they? I want...*

KURT AND ELLIE

It was like a sudden allergic reaction; he was completely fine one minute, but it quickly seized him the next, so intense that it drowned out the indistinct sounds of the bustling bar and the drums and bass emanating from the live band playing in the next room, muffled by the double-brick wall.

The sensation crescendos to white noise, piercing his mind and actualising itself in his stomach as nausea accompanies a cold sweat across his brow. The feeling of pins and needles intensifies rapidly underneath his skin, coursing through each limb. Unable to calm down, focus or breathe regularly—his face is ashen white. He's unwell, but not from anything viral or from something he ate. In a cruddy bathroom stall, twenty-something-year-old Kurtis Neff is in the throes of an anxiety attack.

He tugs on the cuffs of his grey sweater and hastily shuts the toilet lid, sitting. Clenching his cold, clammy hands into a white-knuckled fist, he squeezes tight and desperately prays for relief, but it doesn't come.

'Kurt?' A gentle female voice inquires.

He flinches, taken by surprise. He didn't hear his young wife, Ellie, enter the men's toilet.

'In here.' He responds hesitantly, wincing quietly through clenched teeth.

Ellie discreetly opens the stall door and peaks in to confirm. She finds her husband doubled over on the toilet with his arms crossed and breathing with short, sharp gasps. The shadow of a grimace crosses her face. Kurt spots it, and he wants to believe it's her reaction to the stagnant smell of urine in the air or the misogynistic graffiti branded across the stall walls—not toward him in his current condition. But this scene is all too familiar. This isn't the man Ellie believed in and married just a few short years prior, and although her resentment is triggered, she holds steadfast, assuming this is all just a phase and things between them will get better.

'You okay?'

Kurt manages a smile between shallow breaths. 'Just a little unwell.'

She hides her repulse, takes his hands in hers, looks him straight in his dejected, dark eyes, and attempts to pull him together.

'Everything is fine. You're not sick. We're here now. I'm here.'

'I know, I know.'

'You're going to be fine up there.'

'Yeah, I know. It's not that—really, I'm just—'

'Just what?' Ellie quashes with frustration.

'I'm just unwell, you know and…I think I need to be home and lay on the floor.'

Ellie drops Kurt's hands with a groan.

'Fuck Kurt! You do this every time…we need the money. It's all in your head.'

'You're right. You're right, sorry. I just…I do feel unwell, and I dunno. Do you have any Panadol?'

Irritated, she rummages through her black pleather purse, retrieves a foil blister pack of Panadol and hands it over.

'I'm going back out there,' she declares, leaving the stall.

'I love you,' Kurt replies, using the term as a band-aid.

Paused at the exit, an ugly silence hangs between them. Ellie gazes at her reflection in the bathroom mirror. The moment sparks a memory of advice from a segment of a relationships podcast she once heard: 'Be the type of person you want to be with,' she mumbles, holding back irritated tears, reluctantly offering, 'Love you too,' as she exits.

An odd fear accompanies Kurt's ignorance that he can't quite rationalise. He pops three tablets from the foil blister pack into his palm, and without any water, he swallows them dry. His attention fixates on the back of the wooden stall door, and amongst the countless graffiti tags and scribbled crude jokes is a quote scratched into the back of the wooden door, "THIS IS NOT AN EXIT."

Ellie leans against the bar with a glass of vodka lemon. Her eyes are unmistakably loaded with frustration and sadness. She sweeps a glance around. The bar's alive with Friday evening energy and reasonably crowded with patrons. People order drinks and bartenders expertly pour them while couples converse around tables cluttered with pint and cocktail glasses. The pungent smells of liquor and cigarettes are embedded within the fibres of every element of the bar.

The uninspired "original song" by the twee rock band on stage finally ends. A fresh rack of pool balls breaks as a game kicks off with a squad of lads to Ellie's left. She watches as the green ball, six, enters the corner pocket but questions if it is a nine. Her attention shifts, wandering up along a pool cue held skilfully in the hands of a handsome thirty-something man, a rugged type with broad shoulders you could climb. Poised with precision, he gently and firmly slides the cue back and forth, his eyes locked on the yellow ball. He looks up at Ellie, and she shyly glances away, but only momentarily, as she's drawn back. He offers a warm smile and Ellie returns it politely. With unwavering focus, "Mr. Rugged" pots the ball.

Kurt ascends the stage with an acoustic guitar, his complexion showing signs of recovery. He begins meticulously ensuring his guitar is perfectly in tune. Little to no attention comes his way from any of the patrons. He adjusts the microphone and clears his throat. Ellie's gaze shifts toward the stage as her husband plays a slowed-down, melancholic acoustic rendition of *The Killing Time* by Echo & the Bunnymen.

Mr. Rugged chats with a few mates, turning his back towards Ellie. His mates can't resist a peek past his shoulder in her direction with suggestive cocky gestures to him to "take a crack at her." Although Ellie faces Kurt with a forced smile, she can feel the attention from the billiards squad, particularly Mr. Rugged, who lingers in her peripheral vision. It's been some time since Ellie felt the discomfort of being gawked at, coveted, and objectified—her heart flutters with exhilaration, it excites her.

Ellie's eyes drop to the warm, wet, half-drunken glass in her hand, her ring finger stroking its moisture, and in that fleeting moment, the possibilities of a potential scenario play out in her mind: *Strolling to a discreet corner of the bar, just out of sight, the music fades as Mr. Rugged approaches her and strikes up a flirtatious exchange. She laughs. His blue eyes glisten as he tucks a strand of hair behind her ear and tells her how beautiful and sexy she is. Her lips soften. He pulls her close, and her fingers firmly grasp his Herculean forearms. He moves in and kisses her, then whispers lyrically, "So cruelly you kissed me. Your lips, a magic world." Startled, Ellie pulls away. Mr. Rugged's voice sounds like Kurts...*

Returning to reality—the music amplifies back into focus. Ellie looks back towards the stage, to Kurt, and the complex feelings about their relationship resurface. A sadness ever so subtle, but with roots that reach far and deep, glazes over her eyes.

Kurt's focus shifts towards Ellie: his gaze is fixed. She appears to be studying a guy with a strong brow and jawline, holding a pool cue.

He asks himself, *"Is she checking that juicehead out?"*

Kurt catches the juicehead flash a smile at Ellie, prompting her to look away coyly—the smile plays on her lips. Kurt's legs go numb. He watches the juicehead approach Ellie and talk to her—she giggles. Kurt's mind spirals and catastrophises what was said to cause his wife to elicit such a reaction—a reaction he hasn't seen from her in some time. Distracted by his insecure failings, he misses a note.

A patron seated at a table with her friends looks towards the stage, having detected the off-note. She raises an eyebrow and returns to her friends with a snickering comment.

Ellie stands frozen as Mr. Rugged leans close to speak to her. Her vision blurs and she gazes past him nervously, her attention firmly fixed on Kurt.

Kurt repeatedly sings: "You give yourself to him..." fixated on Ellie and the juicehead.

In that fleeting moment, the possibilities of a scenario play out in his mind: *Ellie cruelly smirks. He drops his guitar, the strings twang, breaking, as he abruptly hops off the stage. A bewildered silence blankets the bar. He stands tall with his head held high and charges past quietly confused patrons towards the juicehead. He taps him on the shoulder. The towering juicehead turns, casting a disdainful glance downward.*

"What're you gonna do about it, Kurt?" Ellie taunts, laughing.

He shoves the juicehead but the hulking beast barely moves, laughing back, fangs menacingly extended. Ellie joins in, laughing. In an abrupt twist, Kurt finds himself clutching his guitar once more. He swings it as hard as he can across the juicehead's arrogant, blood-sucking smile, shattering his teeth. The guitar splinters into pieces, leaving Kurt grasping the jagged neck. Ellie gasps, stunned. Kurt roars, thrusting the broken guitar neck into the juicehead's chest, like a slayer taking down a vampire. Dark, viscous blood violently spews from the gaping wound—

'Give it up, we got it!' Shouts an intoxicated patron from the bar.

Kurt abruptly jolts back to reality and realises he's been playing out of tune. His stomach churns with a cold spell and a hot flush crosses his forehead. He quickly brings the song to an end. Beads of cold sweat roll down his neck as he looks out across the bar.

Awkwardly, he clears his throat and murmurs, 'Thanks,' prudently places his guitar down and steps off stage, stumbling and almost twisting an ankle.

With hunched shoulders, he walks through to the back of the bar, passing awkward faces gawking at him.

Ellie remains poker-faced. Inside, she cringes with "The Ick." judging Kurt as he approaches, mentally urging him to "Just go away."

'Heyyy,' she says, 'you alright?' rubbing his arm. 'See, you did, good.'

He nods, distracted and timidly gawks at the toned arms of the rugged juicehead, who maintains eye contact with Ellie.

'You got great eyes, really big—I love that,' compliments the rugged juice head.

She smiles, awkward and bashful. Kurt is stunned, feeling invisible.

'You still playing, mate?' interrupts the manager from behind the bar.

'Ah…yeah,' replies Kurt.

The bar manager gestures toward the stage, 'Well, do you mind?'

Flustered, Kurt leaves. The feeling of Ellie's touch on his arm still lingers as he heads towards the stage with his tail between his legs. He glances back and catches her expression shift to relief as she looks up at the rugged juicehead. Kurt pauses before the stage platform. The atmosphere of the bar settles into an uneasy silence.

Frozen in thought, his eyes dart, and quietly, under his breath, he mumbles, 'Be the type of person you wanna be with.' His eyes widen as if from a revelation. He sees an image of himself standing tall with his head held high, charging back past confused patrons towards Ellie and the juicehead and knocking him out cold double-quick with a single punch.

Swayed, Kurt looks back and marches right up to the two of them. Ellie appears confused.

'You guys know each other?' the rugged juicehead enquires.

Kurt shifts his gaze to Ellie, expecting her to respond, but she defers back to him—both of them somewhat ashamed, and the silence can be counted across two hands.

'Mate! You playing or not?' interrupts the bar manager once again.

'Just a second,' Kurt mumbles.

'Mate! Either play or fuck off!'

'Kurt!' Ellie pleads.

The rugged juicehead stares at Kurt, waiting.

'We're ma-married,' Kurt stutters.

'Alright, we're done. I'm calling this off,' spits the bar manager impatiently.

'Kurt!' she pleads again.

'She's your wife?' asks the rugged juice head.

She sighs, and the two argue over each other with disjointed sentences. Another awkward silence clouds the air.

'Yeah, right,' replies the rugged juicehead, his confusion tinged with irritation.

Kurt's eyes dart—it's now or never. He shoves the juice head.

She scowls. 'Kurt!'

The rugged juicehead catches his fall along the bench.

'What the fuck!' He exclaims and retaliates, grabbing Kurt's collar.

The two scuffle and in the chaos, Ellie's thwacked against the bar. Losing her balance, she drops her glass. It shatters across the floor. The billiard squad assails Kurt, creating a melee. Suddenly, Kurt is tripped and thrown face-first toward the floor.

Outside, Kurt slams face-first into gravel with a painful thud. His guitar case follows suit, skidding across the ground. Two bouncers behind him at the bar's entrance dust their hands with satisfied grins. Ellie slides out behind them. The bouncers promptly slam the doors shut. Kurt manages to get back to his feet. He's visibly hurt, with a torn shirt and a bloody nose.

Filled with loathing, she looks away as she heads towards the parking lot. 'I can't believe you did that. We needed that money, Kurt.'

He picks up his guitar case and brushes the gravel off. He follows her but keeps his distance.

Ellie whacks the steering wheel. 'Fuck, Kurt! That's not what I meant!' she shouts, keeping her eyes fixed on the dark highway ahead—her hands tighten around the steering wheel.

'What do you mean?' he asks, trying to stem the gushing blood with his head tilted back and fingers pinching his nose.

She groans, shaking her head. Her body aches, screaming—she doesn't want to be here anymore, trapped in this life.

'Just forget it...' she mutters.

Ellie steers their rusty navy 1987 Ford Taurus into their apartment complex. A collection of two-story blocks of brown-bricked square units horseshoe around a cement parking lot with little to no privacy. It's the kind of place where stubborn, creepy old hermits geez with voyeurism, peeking their noses out from behind the drapes as you make your way from the car to the front door.

As the couple drive in, she sits up and leans forward, staring through the windscreen, puzzled. Kurt sees what's caught her attention and knows what will unfold. The couple's belongings, clothes, ornaments, and furniture—everything tossed out of their tiny apartment—lay damaged in their parking space. He begins tugging on the cuffs of his grey sweater, feeling as if his chest is slowly about to implode.

The Taurus squeaks to a gentle halt: the engine idling. Ellie stares dejectedly through the windscreen. Kurt glances toward her with trepidation, expecting another shouting match, but instead, she turns the ignition key, shutting the engine off. Her gaze remains vacant, with an air of defeat. Tears well up, and she begins to cry. He feels his chest sink— the kind of sinking that seems like an immense black hole pulling his world into its vortex and imploding. His mind races, and he questions whether he can say anything to improve the situation, but he knows better.

Ellie exits the car and approaches her belongings piled across the tyre and oil-stained concrete, picking out clothes from the debris of what can only be described as a wardrobe explosion. She takes in the damage of each item and then folds them over one arm.

It dawns upon Kurt to call their landlord and plead their case. He takes out his phone. The number 2 is encapsulated in a red-blaring bubble pinned to the top right-hand corner of the green-boxed phone app. He taps on the app. It reveals one missed voicemail and one missed call from his landlord.

He taps on the voicemail, bringing his phone to his ear and listens to the croaky voice of the landlord barking verbal abuse, "Do you think I was going to let five months go by without a single payment?" he sits on a knife's edge, watching her tearfully collect her belongings from the heaped outcome of their landlord's threats. "I warned you! You hear that?" a clang of something breaking, "That's the sound of eviction, asshole! I'm tossing all ya shit out!" Abruptly, the voicemail disconnects.

Meanwhile, Ellie turns over a broken wardrobe drawer, rummaging inside to retrieve a small antique broach that belonged to her grandmother and was a gift to her on her wedding day. Inside are pictures of him and her on either side, captured in happier times.

Kurt stands beside her tentatively, uncertain if he should place his hand on her shoulder for comfort. He does so anyway and she shrugs him off, closing the brooch with a heavy sigh.

* * *

Another Motel sign emits a glowing red "No Vacancy" as Kurt and Ellie pass by, searching the lonely highway for a place to stay the night. Their Taurus is only packed with what they could squeeze in and strap to the roof.

'What's that, the fifth one now?' she spitefully remarks.

He doesn't bite. The gas symbol on the dash blinks low on fuel. The meter has been dangerously below the line for some time now. He can't ignore it anymore; the last thing he needs to happen is for them to be stuck in the middle of some dark highway. Thankfully, an isolated gas station appears ahead of them; the signage bleeds against the pitch black of the night.

He flicks the indicator. 'I'm gonna get fuel.'

'With what?'

'It's fine. I'm not gonna use what we have left for the motel. I have a twenty in my guitar case.'

'Will that be enough to get us to your mum's place tomorrow?'

He shrugs. 'Should be.'

They pull into the gas station, parking. He gets out and makes his way around to the car trunk. Opening his guitar case, he lifts his Yamaha A5R guitar out and rummages through food wrappers, music sheets, and loose change. He finds the twenty, but it's in two pieces, both crumpled. He pauses, hearing her, and discreetly looks back in. She's crying.

Dismayed and despondent, he turns away, hiding behind the trunk door. Flattening the two pieces of the twenty dollar note, he attempts to paste them together with saliva drooled onto his fingertips and some orange and brown gunk off the side of his guitar case.

Wiping tears from her cheeks, she looks at her reflection in the rear-view mirror, then checks the time on the dashboard. She sighs, annoyed, and unlocks her phone, scrolling through Instagram—images of beautiful women and handsome men. Happy couples. Wealthy couples. Fit couples. Travelling couples. People living out dream lives—all of them influencers selling lies. She hears footsteps and a murmur of voices approaching. Looking out through the windscreen, she sees a happy couple in each other's arms proceeding to the car parked in the next pump station. They separate and get in. The engine starts, and before they drive away, they kiss.

Ellie looks away, then vacantly at her reflection in the rear-view mirror and forces a big smile. Using her two index fingers, she stretches her smiling mouth wider and holds it. Her mouth and cheeks redden. Seconds pass as her eyes well. She releases the flesh, staring at her reflection, and then exits the car.

'Need anything?' She asks.

Kurt shakes his head as he pumps fuel.

'Here.' He says, pointing at the twenty placed upon the roof of the car.

Ellie selects a bottle of Coke Zero from the store fridge and proceeds through the vibrant snack aisle towards the counter, crowded with last-minute automobile supplies and cigarette paraphernalia. The plastic grey CRT television engrosses the stocky shop clerk in front of her above the entrance, blaring a live sports game. She places the Coke Zero on the counter and looks out at her husband, hunched, as he fills their car.

He catches her looking at him, straightening his posture. She coldly averts her gaze. He looks away and sighs.

She looks through the clerk. 'Pump seven, as well.'

The clerk rings it up with stubby but agile fingers, his eyes fixed on the television. Ellie glances over her shoulder to see what's captured his attention.

A lottery commercial with flashy edits and graphics splashes a diverse array of people, grabbing at notes of cash that float falling around them. A quick hard cut to a middle-aged couple lounging on a recliner, wearing goofy-brimmed straw hats and sipping cocktails on an island beach. An immediate star wipe transitions to another man, also middle-aged with a gaping mile-wide smile and porcelain white teeth, grasping a handful of cash with one hand while using his other to drive his new red sports car into the driveway to meet his suburban nuclear family out the front of their new million dollar mansion. Another flashy transition to another cheesy scenario plays out. An overly enthusiastic and annoying voice-over accompanies all of it.

He glances at her. 'One hundred and thirty million dollars! You believe that? They've been playing this ad all night, non-stop. It's the biggest jackpot ever. They're calling it...the dream!'

She looks back and nods, uninterested.

'Everyone's getting a ticket. Even that guy, uh—what's his name? Damn! I can't remember it. Aussie guy—does all those big Hollywood movies.'

'Hugh Jackman?'

'Nah-nah-nah, the angry one.'

'Russell Crowe?'

'Yes!' The clerk clicks with a stubby, pointed finger, 'Gladiator. That's him. Even he came into my store and got a ticket, and he's loaded.'

She looks deadpan at him, 'Hmm. So, can I pay for my stuff?'

His high-spirited expression flattens—extinguished by a young woman in a lousy mood with a resting bitch face.

She hands him the twenty, and it comes apart as he tugs at it. He holds one half. She holds the other: surprised, unaware and embarrassed.

'What is this?'

Ah…' she hands him the other half.

He holds the two ends of a twenty-dollar note in each hand. 'What am I supposed to do with this?'

She glances out the storefront window at Kurt, now seated inside the car. He taps on his wrist, indicating she should hurry up. She frowns, annoyed.

'Can't you tape it together?'

'It's void. The bank won't take this.'

'Won't they? I'm sure they would if you asked them nicely.'

He slams both pieces on the counter and slides them back to her. 'You better be able to pay for the fuel.'

'Ah—yes. Yes, I got it… Here,' holding out a debit card from her purse.

He hands her the EFT device. She taps her card, and a moment passes as the device displays a 16-bit style graphic of a satellite signal travelling from the machine to a building. The machine alarms with a chime. "Insufficient funds."

'Shit. Can I try that again?'

Unamused and with a crooked frown, he dials it up again and hands the device back to her. She taps, and the device again chimes. "Insufficient funds."

Quickly, she takes out another card, 'Sorry. I meant to try this one?'

His patience wanes with a deep sigh, redialling the device. Ellie taps. It chimes, but this time, the payment is successful. She sighs with relief.

He gestures towards the television. 'Maybe you could use some luck? If you win, you and your husband won't need to argue about money.'

'Excuse me?' she asks, caught off guard.

'Don't worry, I've been married a few times now. I know an argument about money when I see it,' he gestures toward the couple's vehicle outside, crammed with their belongings, 'especially a couple on vacation.'

She looks out the shop front window, disheartened, and quietly states, 'We're not on vacation.'

'What's that?' he asks.

'We're not on—it doesn't matter. So how much is a ticket anyway?'

'Eighteen dollars.'

She sighs and thinks for a moment. 'Fuck it, why not! What's another eighteen dollars on an already inflated credit card anyway.'

She waits as he rings it up.

'Maybe if you win tonight, you can go on vacation,' he hands the lottery ticket over.

She takes it and turns to exit.

'Life could be a dream,' he declares loudly.

Ellie halts under the exit doors and looks back over her shoulder. He enthusiastically points to the television above her. She looks up at the screen—the lottery ad plays again—a star wipe to a happy couple, strangely not too dissimilar to her and Kurt. Mystified, she looks back at him. He beams a smile, nodding. She nods hesitantly and then exits.

The rural highway stretches endlessly, dimly lit, devoid of traffic, with no motel in sight. Kurt grips the steering wheel, his gaze fixed ahead, while Ellie takes occasional sips from her Coke Zero. The sweltering heat adds to the unspoken and unsettled tension hanging between them, but their inner voices have plenty to say to each other. She presses the air-con button on and off with a flurry of frustration, knowing full well that it's broken—a passive aggressive statement.

Fed up with the oppressive silence, Ellie switches on the

car radio. The final stretch of *A Different Gun* by Johnny Marr plays, filling the car with its haunting melodies. The digital clock on the dashboard illuminates 19:57.

She reaches into her black pleather purse, retrieving the recently purchased lottery ticket and a worn BIC ballpoint pen in black. Its cap bears the battle scars of nervous chewing. Kurt sneaks a glance in her direction.

'You bought a lottery ticket?'

'Yeah, so?'

He returns his attention to the road, but the idea gnaws at him. "A lottery ticket?" he thinks, unable to shake it off.

'You know the chances of winning are like one in twenty million or something,' he squawks. 'It's a scam!'

'What I do with my money is my business.'

'Oh! Your money? What happened to our money?'

'Ha! What did happen to our money, Kurt? Like, the fucking rent! Five months, Kurt!' she exclaims. 'Where did it go?' throwing her hands up in frustration.

'I already told you—'

'You blew our money on your bullshit again, is what happened! I can't believe we've been evicted!'

'So, my music is bullshit now?'

'Ugh! No. I didn't mean it like that. You know I care about your music—'

'No, I get it. Really!'

Ellie shakes her head in disbelief, gazing out the passenger-side window.

'It costs money to record, you know,' he continues, 'I'm so close—I mean, like, things will change. Just need that one fucking break…I thought you understood that.'

She glances back to the dashboard, the time: 20:02, and gently raises the volume on the radio.

"*…live across the nation, it's The Dream Jackpot, Mega Lotto! It's Boxing Day, December 26th. I'm Camila Peña, bringing tonight's winning numbers to the largest jackpot draw ever. A One*

Hundred and Fifty Million Dollars! Talk about ringing in the new year..."

Kurt sneers with an ugly chuckle, but she pays no attention, leaning forward to listen with anticipation.

"Let's not waste any more time. One lucky winner is out there waiting for their life to change. Our first winning number tonight is 42, that's followed by 26, up next we have 60, your next number is 51, and your final number is 4..."

She hastily jots the numbers on her hand.

"Now for the mega lotto dream number... that number is 8. Again, tonight's winning numbers are 42, 26, 60, 51, 4 and the dream number 8. Good luck out there!"—The radio play transitions to a song, *Fall Out* by The Police. Kurt twists a dial, lowering the radio volume.

Ellie stares at the ticket in her hand, her head slightly tilts, daydreaming, already spending the potential winnings: *a beach house with a view and overseas travel; walking the streets of Rue Saint Honoré Paris and Manhattan's Fifth Avenue clutching shopping bags from designer stores...* She snaps out of it and eagerly checks her ticket against the numbers on the back of her hand, circling a few numbers: 26, 51, 4.

'Well?' Kurt asks with a glance.

She scans the square grid of random numbers with her black BIC. Her enthusiasm dwindles. She stops and remains still and quiet. Vulnerable. She suddenly twitches, crumpling the ticket into a tight ball, staring ahead at the dark, empty highway with bereaved eyes and a bitter glare. And like so many others, she will spend another night with a deadbeat husband and shattered dreams from a losing lottery ticket.

Kurt glances her way again, the slightest of smirks lingering on his face, the kind most people would want to smack.

Less than a kilometre ahead, a set of bright red taillights suddenly veer off the left side of the desolate two-lane highway.

Ellie double-takes and winces with a worried expression. 'Did you see that?'

He refocuses his attention on the road ahead. 'See what?'

'Ahead of us—a car.'

'What car?'

'There was a car ahead of us. The taillights,' she gestures, waving her hands, 'they went wonky—I think it crashed.'

'Wonky?'

'Just slow down. We're coming up to it.'

'We're on a highway. I can't just slow—'

'Slow down! Slow down!'

Kurt reluctantly decreases their speed from eighty to fifty.

'Look!' she points out the passenger side as they pass slowly.

Off the side of the highway, they spot a pair of faint red taillights and a glimpse of a crumpled vehicle shrouded within the darkness of bushland.

'Oh, shit! That just happened?' he exclaims.

'Didn't you see it go off the road?'

'I was looking at you!'

'What do we do?' she asks with growing concern.

The Taurus decelerates to a crawl, eventually pulling to a halt off the side of the highway. Its hazard lights blink. The vehicle proceeds to reverse for half a kilometre back down the road before finally coming to a halt. It sits idling, the engine humming quietly.

Kurt looks at Ellie as she peers out the passenger window, focused on the obscured red taillights of the crashed vehicle. He seeks her input and awaits her decision about what to do next, but she returns a look of uncertainty, urging him to make the next call. He probes the rear-view mirror and shifts his attention out of the windscreen. The little clarity the headlights cast on the dark road indicates no sight of any oncoming traffic. He reaches for the ignition key; his hand trembles with uneasy resolve, shutting the engine off. It falls into silence with the blinking hazard lights and the faint thrum of the night.

THE DRUM

I wake up suddenly but sluggishly. My eyes are heavy. I take a deep breath—an announcement over the P.A. informs me the next station will be Carlton. I sit up and try to clear my head… *Carlton?* I walk to the door and look at the rail map fixed on the carriage wall. Hurstville's only a couple of stops away. *Heh, what're the chances?*

I look out the window and at an intersection of the street, I notice a white, late 90s Toyota Rav4. It takes off at a green light and I notice the licence plate has the number 111 on it. *Hey Angel.* It reminds me of her, and it makes me smile. Angel numbers and green lights…and then this train turns out to be the right one to get me to Hurstville. I take it as a sign. Angel would tell me about signs, saying they were messages of assurance that you're heading in the right direction: on the right path. *What'd she call it?… expansion in consciousness, or was it expansion of the soul?* Either way, she was into that sorta thing. I didn't know much about any of that, not that I know much now. I just loved listening to her talk about it. I figured she was giving me a message. That's what angels do.

* * *

I'm in Hurstville, but I underestimated the walk to the Drum. That's where I'm going: to see an old friend, and for my sake, I hope she's still there. The Drum is a little-known brothel located in an unsuspecting two-story townhouse not too far off the highway. It sits discreetly nestled amongst several warehouses and used car lots off an industrial street, secured with a 7ft Colorbond steel fence, razor wire and pine trees behind a busy petrol station. It's where I worked as a bouncer, keeping the girls safe from undersexed assholes and entitled twenty-something-year-olds celebrating a little too long into the early hours of the morning. You can disappear there without knowing it. It's also where Angel worked, but that isn't where I met her.

The smell of lamb wafts through the air, which means I'm not far, just around the corner. The sickening smell of over-cooked lamb is from a kebab truck on the side of a service station's parking lot. Not the sexiest of smells when paying for your dick to get wet.

I stand out front, and since I last saw her, the Drum's seen better days. I head round back, not wanting to knock on the main entrance or the discrete entrance to the side, knowing where the CCTV cameras are. I can avoid being seen. I don't want anyone to know I'm here. A fire escape ladder was installed a few months before my last shift.

I keep quiet and slowly climb to the second floor. There, between two Venetian-like windows, a curtain is draped from the inside. If I remember correctly, it should be the one on the left: Angel's room was on the right. It occurs to me that I haven't removed the bandages from my neck or attempted to talk. I sit against the railing and unwind the sweaty bandages. I feel the scars underneath. They're like burns but healed, so I'm unsure what the dressing was for. Maybe the skin's fragile and thin. Maybe it looks bad. Maybe the nurses got sick at the sight of me. I won't know for sure till I get a look at it. I clear my throat, and it feels better than when I vomited earlier.

'Hey.' I gasp.

I moisten my mouth and try again. 'Hey.' *That feels a little better.* 'Sorry to drop in.' That hurt...*and I sound stupid.* But I can work through it. Nothing a little homemade tea from your mother couldn't fix...or whisky forced down ya throat from an abusive father—*either way.*

'Hey, it's...' I pause.

I can't say my name. I don't know why I can't say it. I know my name, but I have this sudden feeling of sadness. No —I can't feel sad, can't feel sorry for myself. Not now—not ever. Not for Angel.

I get up and lean out towards the window and tap, waiting. Half a minute passes, so I reach out and tap again, this time a little harder and louder. I lean back against the ladder and wait. After a moment, someone brushes the curtains to one side, and I see a blond girl I ain't ever seen before peering out. I keep braced against the ladder to her left, out of sight. The curtains close, and the girl is gone.

Damn. I didn't want to, but I'm 'ere...maybe, just maybe.

I lean out and to the right window, Angel's old room. Fortunately, there's a slim gap between the curtains, and I peer through. I see a familiar girl, cross-legged on the floor, leaning forward at a mirror resting against the wall facing away from me, fixing her dark eyeliner along her Sanpaku eyes. Her hair is now in a bob-cut and splits in two colours: purple and a deep pink, which makes me second guess. But no other girls I remember here would dare to wear a short green tartan skirt and black stockings outside a client's request. She's also wearing an oversized faded black "Karnivool" band t-shirt with Doc Marten boots—*gotta be her.* I take my chances and tap the window. Hearing it, she pauses. I tap again. I don't want her to think she's crazy, hearing things. She turns towards the window, and I see her face properly. It's her. I wave, tap again, and she approaches the window. Quickly, she pulls back the curtains, and upon seeing me, gasps, startled. I smile. I can only imagine how awkward I look doing so. She unhinges the lock on the window and opens it.

'Frank?'

'Hey Candy.'

I stand inside Angel's room. At least it used to be. I hold Candy's slight, 5'3" body in my arms, embracing her as she pours out emotion, crying for her best friend and the love of my life: our Angel. But I can't do this, not right now. I gently pull away. I know she'll ask me, and I'll have to tell her the little I know. But not now.

I play dumb and make an obvious statement, 'You moved into her room.'

She nods slowly. 'The thought of one of the new girls moving in felt wrong. I didn't think Angel would mind.'

I smile. 'Nah, she wouldn't have.'

'I kept all her stuff! But none of her clothes fit me.'

I smile again: a new record. I remember a time when Candy tried on a new outfit Angel had bought over a black Friday weekend and how they laughed, giggling like a couple of teenagers at how ridiculous she looked wearing it.

Candy and Angel were popular and highly requested but for different reasons. Candy's in her mid-twenties, but rather petite and doesn't look a day over sixteen. She fulfils the little girl fantasy: the naughty student or naive stepdaughter. And Angel, well... I can't speak to it and never asked because I didn't care to know what she used to do for her clients. None of my business. I can only speak to what I know, to what we knew, to what we shared, but I've never been the kiss-and-tell type. Anyway, that's the kind of stuff the Drum offers. Fantasies. It's clean, high-end, and one of the best-kept secrets in Sydney.

I pick up an 8x10 frame with a picture of a happy little boy from Candy's bedside table.

'Oscar?'

She looks at the picture, offering a small, sad smile. 'Had his tenth birthday just last week… I couldn't make it. Mum says he's getting tall.'

I smile for a third time, apparently making a habit out of it and return the frame.

'That's great.'

Everyone's heard Candy's story before because it's an unfortunate trope that happens too often to be anything but accurate. A curious young girl from a conservative family gets knocked up, but not because she's promiscuous. No, it was her uncle—I think he was a pastor—another man in a position of power taking advantage. No one believed her. They blamed her and shunned her, and she became a runaway looking for a home. She wound up here.

Candy sits on the edge of her bed and watches me float through Angel's room—her room, taking in the changes since I was last here. I point to a dresser draped with a cloth on which Celtic text and symbols are etched. Ritually positioned on it are lit candles, a sage bowl and the crystals tourmaline, obsidian, and tiger's eye.

I nod at it. 'This is new.'

'You know you look like shit,' she says bluntly, 'sorry, it's just—'

'It's fine,' I say, cutting her off. I take a breath. I forgot how blunt she can be.

'I visited a few times… nurses said I was wasting my time. Said you would never wake up again.'

They were almost right. The state of being in a coma is like death adjacent.

I smirk and change the subject. 'You know—I could really use a shave and a haircut.'

She smiles. 'Let me get the scissors.'

We swap positions. I sit on the edge of her bed, but she moves into the en suite, calling me in. She stands in the bathtub, waiting with scissors and a comb. I enter and sit, facing away from her on the edge of the tub and lean back a little, but before she gets to work, I suddenly feel a sickness over-whelm me and I become dizzy. I stand up and turn to her.

'You okay?' she asks.

My vision tunnels, blurring, and I collapse.

I stare up at Candy from the floor. She's panicked, shouting my name and I feel a warm oozing form across my brow. The bathroom dims, fading to black.

* * *

I wake up slowly. My vision's blurry. I gaze at a shadowy corner of the ceiling in Angel's room...Candy's room. I feel dry with a sore throat and foggy brain, like the morning of a hangover, on a couple of hours of sleep.

Candy leans in and replaces a cloth from across my brow.

'Frank?' Madame Lacey leans in alongside her, arms crossed. 'Son of a bitch!'

'Mum, please—not now,' asks Candy.

I sit up, catching the cloth as it falls from my brow. 'What happened?'

'What happened?' Madame Lacey rebukes, 'you break in and pass out for sixteen hours. I had to cancel several of Candy's clients. What the hell are you even doing back here anyway?'

'He didn't break in, mum,' murmurs Candy.

'Sixteen hours?' I ask, scratching my head. I feel a bandage.

Fed up, Madame Lacey stalks to the door in a huff, 'I have to manage the desk,' but she pauses and looks back at me, 'You look like shit... eat a sandwich, get some rest.' She leaves the room, shutting the door behind her.

'You hit your head. It was bleeding, so I wrapped it.' Candy tells me.

'So, does that mean I can stay?'

'You know what she's like, just doesn't want any trouble.'

Madame Lacey, old school of hard knocks she is. The girls

here call her mum, mother hen, but never warden; that title's reserved for the staff. There's a knock at the door and it creeps open. Speaking of staff, Nicky enters with a mug of coffee, a plate of toasted sandwiches and a side of fries. It's exactly what I need.

'Hey Frank,' Nicky smiles, happy to see an old friend, 'heard you were back from the dead!'

Candy frowns with a raised eyebrow.

'Uh, joking,' he says sheepishly.

'Good to see you too, bud,' I say with a wink.

Nicky takes care of the bar, and he's good at his job cause he likes what he does. Sweet kid with a big heart: always sees the best in folks and doesn't have a judgmental bone in his body, even towards the Drum's scumbag clients. I guess that's how he's able to work here. Girls love him for it too. Imagine Jimmy Olsen and Peter Parker had a kid, that's Nicky, but Italian.

'So you gonna stick around, Frank?'

I finish chugging hot coffee and wipe my mouth. 'I don't mean to be rude, but I'm just not in the mood to answer questions right now.'

With bated breath, the kid stands looking at me—an awkward silence hangs between us all. 'Hey, Nicky, maybe you could get us some fruit or something? Something fresh might be better?' suggests Candy.

He nods eagerly. 'Oh, of course—yeah, great idea. I'll be right back!'

'More coffee too.' I tell him.

The kid turns back, nods and dashes out the door. Like I said, sweet kid. I try to stand up but fall ass backwards on the bed.

'Where do you think you're going?' asks Candy.

I lay light-headed and without an answer.

She shakes her head. 'You've been asleep for some time.'

I nod and she tells me the truth, 'So what's a few more days? Take mum's advice, eat and get some rest. Get your strength back.' She takes the empty mug from my hand and lifts my feet onto the pillow. 'I'll get some more blankets.' I lay back, staring at the ceiling. My attention drifts to the cracks in the paint along the skirting. My eyes feel heavy again.

* * *

Several days and thirty protein shakes later, I'm seated at the Drum's oval kitchen table, out back, scoffing a scotch fillet—medium rare, with a sourdough baguette. It's 2AM and Madame Lacey strolls in. No makeup, I ain't ever seen her without it and her hair's in a bun. I sit and swallow my food.

'How're the shoes?' She asks.

Some geezer left his shoes, running out, caught by his old lady who followed him.

'Tight, but they'll do.'

She pours a cup of tea and takes a seat beside me.

I pick at my bread. 'Why do I feel like a kid in trouble whenever I'm around you?'

'I've known plenty of men like you. They always bring trouble.'

'I've always found trouble finds me.'

'Same difference.'

'Is that why you don't like me?'

'I don't *not* like you. I don't like trouble.'

'Why did you ever hire me to watch over the girls?'

'I didn't hire you to watch over the girls, I employed you to watch over the clients.'

'You know what I mean.'

She sips from her cup. 'I take what I can get.'

I tear another piece of bread and chew on it, watching Madame Lacey sip her tea. 'Kinda ironic, don't you think? You not wantin' any trouble, yet you run a whorehouse.'

She stands up. 'You watch what you say about this place. It's been good to people. I've been good to people, including you. Girls like Candy need this place...and Angel did too.'

Then she drops a bombshell on me. 'Who do you think kept paying for the hospital to prevent them from pulling the plug on you?'

'What?' *Candy?*

'Asshole.' She takes her cup to the sink, pours out what remains and heads toward the door.

'Wait! You didn't answer my question.'

She pauses. 'You didn't ask a question; you made a statement, a stupid one at that,' she glances over her shoulder at me, 'as I said, I take what I can get,' and leaves.

* * *

I splash away the remaining offcuts of my beard down the basin drain and turn the tap off. Wiping the condensation from the bathroom mirror, I stare back at myself with familiar eyes—my eyes. They've never changed. My face is clean-shaven, with my hair cut and combed back. The scars on my face and neck are clearer. I touch them and follow them from one point to the other. One line of scarring begins from the back of my neck, just behind my ear, then comes underneath and around to my left eye. Strange that whatever cut me decided to pass around my ear.

I hear Candy crying. She asked me bluntly about what happened, but this time, with scissors at my throat. I let her do it because I knew she couldn't go ahead with it, but I wanted her to. She's a complex girl and doesn't trust men much—even me. So, I told her about the crash, those two kid's and what I believe they did to Angel. That's why she's crying in the other room. Now she knows.

I leave the bathroom with only a towel wrapped around my waist. Candy sits on a chaise lounge at the end of her bed, she looks at me, wiping away tears. Shocked, her jaw drops a little at the sight of my body, riddled with bed sores and bruises.

She catches herself staring, and softly says, 'Sorry.'

I smile. 'It's okay.'

Looking away, she points to her dresser. 'There're clothes in a box at the bottom there.'

I take the box out and bring it to the bed, finding a pair of blue jeans and a pastel-coloured shirt. I try them on. The jeans are oversized around my waist. The tag reads 38; usually, that would be fine, but I've got nothing on me. I must be down to 29 or 30.

'I'm gonna need a belt.'

'Oh—yeah—I got one,' she says, going to her dresser. Rummaging through a drawer, she takes out a dark brown leather belt and passes it to me. It has a large silver belt buckle. The image on the buckle is of a horse frozen mid-gallop. I admire the details of the image and how free the horse appears. I feel Candy watching me while trying not to at the same time. I say nothing, but I am curious about what she's thinking. I strap the belt around me, followed by the pastel shirt. It's also big on me, so I roll the sleeves up.

'I'm sorry about the scissors,' she offers.

'Don't be.'

I see Polaroids of Angel tacked around the edge of her mirror. I walk over. I haven't seen them before; she must have put them up. They capture Angel as I remember her: happy, fun-loving, always smiling and laughing. I haven't had a chance to miss her. One picture sticks out. It's of us, happily caught by surprise just outside the door to this room. I glance back at Candy.

'I miss her so much,' she admits, tears rolling down her cheeks.

I sit on the short chaise lounge and put my arm around her. She cuddles up to me. A deep sadness consumes my chest. I close my eyes. The smiling image of Angel from the Polaroid is still fresh in my mind. It's the same smile Angel greeted me with on our last Christmas together.

'TWAS THE NIGHT BEFORE CHRISTMAS

Frank reclines on his living room's beige carpet. 6'1", shirtless with a solid build, he has a wispy streak of grey hair like smoke from a cigarette, and unless you're told, you can't quite figure out where his enigmatic dark features originate. He stares at the ceiling fan steadily whirling, his mind wandering until interrupted by the ring of a mobile phone. He sits up and answers. A smirk plays across his lips, hearing the voice on the other end.

'On my way,' Frank replies.

As he leaves his apartment, he throws on a shabby black denim trucker jacket before pausing at his fish tank. He opens a fresh packet of shrimp flakes with a cheerful cartoon grinning goldfish on the label and sprinkles them across the water's surface. Several goldfish swarm swiftly to the surface.

'Merry Christmas guys.'

As he approaches the lift in the hallway, he sees a crudely handwritten sign taped across the stainless-steel doors that reads, "Out of Order", and without hesitation, he bypasses it, taking the stairs several floors down.

Upon reaching the ground level, Frank stops at his mailbox and sorts through a bunch of keys and a pair of dog tags looped together with half a shoelace. He finds the small, rusting key he wants, and with a deft twist, unlocks the mail-box. He removes a bundle of envelopes held together with a red elastic band. Perusing the mostly junk mail with a quick shuffle, he pockets the only one with a stamp and hand-written address in his jacket and exits.

* * *

The city glistens like a sea of twinkling Christmas lights in Frank's rear-view mirror. He veers off the highway and passes beneath an exit sign that reads: "Hurstville." Ahead of him is The Drum.

Frank guides his vehicle up the driveway and navigates to a small ten-spot parking lot at the back, neatly parking between two other cars. He steps out and makes his way toward the back door of the Drum, illuminated by a solitary red globe overhead. Frank glances up at the surveillance camera and politely salutes before waiting.

The door's lock releases with a hard click and swings open. Rongo and Aata greet him with a bro handshake-hug; they're two Māori brothers with tāmoko tattoos. They step aside, revealing a captivating 27-year-old woman with hands on her hips. She's tall with slender legs that go all the way up into firm-fitted Levi's shorts. The elastics of her hot pink panties peek out just above the waistband, just as the bra straps do underneath her white singlet. Her thick blonde hair accentuates her heart-shaped face and soft green eyes. She greets him eagerly with a smile.

Frank smirks back, 'Hey Angel.'

She joyfully bounds up to him and he embraces her warmly. Her legs wrap around his waist as she peppers him with affectionate kisses.

Inside, the lobby is warm and dimly lit. Frank carries Angel through, her legs still wrapped around him. *I Want to Come Home for Christmas* by Marvin Gaye serenades the room. The walls of the lobby are painted with red velvet. Beautiful black and white portraits of famous and notorious women are hung throughout: Debbie Harry, Lynn Rovner and a mugshot of Laura Bullion.

Several men, some in suits with cocktails, sit accompanied by attractive women on comfortable sofas and throw pillows. Some of the working girls dress formally in glittery cocktail dresses, while others dress scantily in lingerie and thigh-high stockings.

Frank and Angel pass through, heading towards the staircase. 'Hey Frank!' a familiar voice calls out.

Frank looks to the hole-in-the-wall wine bar, where Nicky, classily garbed, pours a martini for a standing patron and cheerfully gestures. 'I didn't know you're bouncing Christmas Eve tonight.'

'He's not. He's with me tonight, and it's his birthday,' replies Angel.

'You were born on Christmas Eve?' asks Nicky.

Frank shrugs and with a smile, takes Angel upstairs.

'Well, Merry Christmas and a Happy Birthday!' chuckles Nicky.

Upstairs, with Angel still in his arms, they head down the second-floor hallway, which has several rooms on either side. Just as they're about to enter Angel's room, Candy, with long, dyed black hair and wearing an oversized "TOOL" band T-shirt, surprises them with a snap from her Polaroid.

'Smile!'—the camera goes CLICK-WHIRR, spitting out a white framed picture.

Angel and Frank smile, laughing, temporarily blinded by the camera's intense flash.

Candy plucks the picture from the camera's mouth and places it into Frank's. 'Happy Birthday, Franky.'

Frank winks and Angel smiles as they turn inside her room.

'Oh! And guys, try to not make too much noise.' Candy winks cheekily as the door slowly closes on her. Stepping away, she leans back against the railing, lost in thought, longing for a day when—

'Candy?' Interrupts Madame Lacey from the lobby, 'Are you ready?'

Leaning over the railing, Candy replies, irked, 'Yes, mum,' and dashes down the hallway.

Heavy panting accompanies hungry kisses and beading sweat on naked skin. Frank and Angel make love in the periodic soft red neon sign glitching outside from the nearby petrol station, washing over them like an emergency siren, silhouetting Frank and Angel's perfectly cut bodies in the dark, thrusting to a vigorous climax.

They lay half naked in each other's arms, bedsheets partially draped over them. Moonlight fills the room now that the red neon sign has completely fused out. Angel sits up and steps out, passing over their clothes, scattered across the floor and over to a mini-fridge where she gathers a couple of cold pilsners. She opens them and sinks back a mouthful.

Noticing an envelope with Frank's name handwritten in cursive poking out of his leather jacket's pocket, hanging on the back of a wooden desk chair, she strolls over, plucks it out and turns to him. 'Secret lover?'

'Nah, grandmother…birthday card. You can open it.'

She opens the envelope. Inside, as Frank said, is a birthday card, a kooky children's one with a retro-future cartoon robot.

His grandmother signed the card with a message, "To my beautiful boy". Scotch-taped to the opposite side is a lottery ticket. Angel chuckles.

'What's so funny?' he asks.

'Your gran gifts you a lottery ticket?'

'It's just somethin' she's always done,' he shrugs.

'And the funny card?'

'A silly dream she still holds on to for me.'

She places the beers on the bedside table and slides back into bed alongside him, burying her head in his chest. 'Can I ask about your parents?'

'Really?'

'Yes-really, I've only ever heard you mention your gran... said you would.'

'Does that day have to be now?...there isn't much to say.'

'Nothing at all?'

He shakes his head.

'Well, our long car rides together are going to be awfully quiet.'

He doesn't respond.

'If we're gonna run away together, you'll need to be a little more talkative. It doesn't need to be your life story. Just start small.'

He thinks for a moment. 'Okay...' adjusting his position and thinking some more. 'As I got older, I saw my old man for what he really was and realised I had nothin' in common with him. He was a liar and a coward...and I was too honest.'

Angel's eyes sparkle with adoration. 'You are honest. I can imagine, little honest Franky. What about your mum?'

Frank shrugs. 'She's dead...I was alongside her on her deathbed, but I was too late to make amends. She didn't do nothin' wrong. I mean, she was no saint, but she sure as hell was no sinner either. Nah, that was my ol' man... god, she tried to leave sooner and take me with her, but, my ol' man caught on, countered her and the next day we're headin' north of Victoria without her. Didn't see her again for twenty-somethin' years. Yeah... you see, my ol' man got into my head too when I was a kid and fucked my perception of things... the world, women and the way I felt towards my Mum. He made me believe she was weak and pathetic—an example of the world and its failures. Hyper-narcissist shit. Convinced me of cuttin' her out of my life, so good that I didn't even realise... He made me hate her.'

Angel squeezes his hand.

'Nah, I fucked up.'

'Baby… that's not your fault.'

He glances at her. 'Yeah.'

'No, baby…It's not your fault. It's his, it's your dad's fault. You were an innocent, impressionable little kid. Children trust their parents. You trusted your father, and he took advantage of that. He abused your innocence. He abused you.'

'Nah-yeah, I know.'

Silence settles. He stares out into nothing, feeling her eyes on him. 'Yeah, I know, really.'

'Where's your dad now?'

'Alone in some beige-walled old folks' home, rottin' away… I figure it's only fair.'

Sitting up, she offers cheekily, 'And I thought daddy issues were only reserved for gals like me,' in an attempt to lighten the mood. It works, forcing him to smirk.

'See, that wasn't so hard now, was it?' she quips, 'I think I'd like to hear about this dream your granny has for you. I doubt it's one where you're in an unconventional relationship with a working girl.'

He reaches for his beer. 'You know I don't care about that,' kissing her forehead as he picks it up, taking a swig. It's quiet and he's lost in his thoughts.

She slaps his arm gently. 'Hey, I'm serious. I want to know.'

He shrugs. 'It's stupid.'

She looks at him, endearingly. 'I really want to know. I promise I won't make fun,' and she sits up: all ears, waiting for his response.

Frank sighs. 'I used to write and draw—like comic books n' science fiction—Robots and future worlds, that kinda thing…I even went to an art school for a bit… My gran still holds onto that old idea of me, believin' that one day, I'd…I dunno, write a book or somethin'.'

'Aww, your gran sounds sweet. I hope I get to meet her someday. So, do you still write?'

He takes another swig. 'Sometimes. I haven't been… disciplined.'

'So getting you a journal for your birthday would be a good idea then?—You know, to help your discipline.'

His eyes narrow. 'I don't journal. Life so far has been…,' and he lowers his head, not ready to share, 'I just prefer fiction for now.'

Angel looks away. 'Oh…'

He pauses mid-way through another swig, realising and turns to her. 'Did you—'

She surprises him with a journal, gift-wrapped with a bow. 'Happy birthday Franky baby.'

'Oh Angel, I didn't mean to—'

She slides a long, delicate finger over his lips. 'It's okay, I know. I believe you have a story in you, and when the time is right, you'll be able to write it.'

He nods, giving her a gentle smile and leans forward kissing her.

She breaks their lip-lock, radiating excitement. 'Well, open it.'

He takes the gift from her hands, pulls on the bow, and tears the wrapping away, revealing a pocket-sized leather-bound journal, dark brown and about an inch thick. Opening the cover, he sees inside, centred on the opening page above several cursive XOXOs, are simply the words "Happy Birthday."

He looks at her sheepishly and kisses her tenderly, thanking her.

Laid back in each other's arms again, Angel plays with the dark hair on Franks's chest, curling it around her finger.

'Tell me about one of your stories.'

He grimaces, exhaling.

She prods him with an elbow. 'You're so full of resistance tonight! C'mon, I wanna hear.'

He sighs again.

'And will you stop sighing like a spoiled brat?' she snaps.

'Alright—alright,' he thinks for a moment. 'I got this one story that I've sat on for far too long. It's about a robot meetin' this newly cloned woman, and they form a connection...a bond! They'll fall in love...but! They're also on the run, havin' to escape across the county lookin' for humanity.'

A silence hangs as he waits expectantly for her reaction. 'Well?'

'I love it!' she replies, looking at him adoringly.

'Yeah—really?'

'Yeah. Really. Do you have a title for it?'

'Nah, I'm terrible with things like that.'

She rolls to her side, taking his arm to spoon her tightly. They stare into nothingness, silently lost in thought.

He swigs more beer and looks down at her. 'What're you thinkin' about?'

'Oh, you know. Everything.'

'Everythin'?'

'Everything.'

'You wanna be more specific?'

'Sure, but... I don't know if you want to hear it.'

'Now, who's being resistant? I asked, didn't I?'

'Well...I think about people...where they are, and what they do. I think about the people in the streets and people in their homes. The things they eat and the things they wear. I think about the people they love and how they love them. I think about the men and women who come and see me. I think about the masks they wear and their performance in their daily lives, the sadness behind their eyes, and the lengths they go to keep it up. I think about how they seek therapy, spirituality, religion, entertainment, ideology, and law. And despite all that, they still come and see me—leaving all that shit at the door. Their little Angel—where they can take off their masks and rest from their performances, I think about…everything,' she turns to face him, but her eyes don't settle on his, gazing around his face, 'and then I think about me being here with you and how I leave all my shit at the door—where I don't have to perform and can rest and be myself—with you…' she settles her gaze on his eyes, 'in love.'

Frank's silenced, staring into the eyes of an angel. He leans in to meet her lips.

They kiss, eyes closed tight, and he pleads, praying to whoever's listening, "Don't take her away from me! Not ever! Not this one—please don't." …

Frank gently opens his eyes but suddenly pulls away, eyes wide —shocked and frightened at the sight of Angel. She lies lifeless in his arms. Her complexion is sickly pale, blue and green. Her eyes are bloodshot, and her hair is matted wet with grass, mud and rat-tailed maggots. She groans, drooling blood. Frank drops her limp body, screaming, scared. Vertigo hits him.

HOWLING AT A FULL MOON

Frank's vision spins—he jumps out of bed, standing naked. The environment surrounding him is now bushland. A cold flush falls across his brow: he's nauseous, falling to his knees, dry reaching— the sounds of women orgasming, panting and moaning drone against the rising noise of buzzing flies. Frank looks up towards the stalks of surrounding trees and sees Angel's bed hoisted: the under- sheet is stained with a grid of numbers written in blood, and she is naked and crucified upon it. Two grey figures appear alongside as the bed lowers. The shadowy figures hold mallets and their faces are blurry, but to Frank, they're the two kids, Ellie and Kurt. They begin to hammer large rose thorns into Angel's body.

Frank shivers, helpless, shackled by heavy chains leading into the ground underneath him. A beady-eyed crow perched on top of a pike stares at him, watching the chains rattle and then draw, pulling him underneath the foundation that has now become a dense, soupy marsh. In a horrified panic and with the swamp at his neck, Frank takes his last breath and cries, "Not yet."

I jerk, waking up panicked in a cold sweat, grasping my chest —*another goddamn nightmare.*

'Christ.'

I'm lying on the chaise lounge at the end of Candy's bed. I sit up, confused.

Candy sits at a small fold-out table draped in a red velvet cloth with several lit candles. The smell of nag champa incense is in the air. She pulls a tarot card from an ornate deck and lays it next to five others.

I crack my neck. 'How long was I sleepin' for?'

'Only a couple of hours. I ordered some pizza. It's just on the bed behind you. Hopefully, it's not too cold. Capriccioso with artichokes instead of anchovies, right?'

'Yeah,' I look behind and lift the pizza box lid, 'thanks,' I take a slice and start eating. 'Beers are in the fridge too,' she says, turning towards me, 'why did you come here? What I mean is….'

I cut her off, 'It's okay—don't worry about it.'

The moment it takes to swallow my food allows me to contemplate what I shouldn't say or plan to do.

Can't go telling people I'm out for blood. 'I want information about the crash.' *Which is true.*

She gestures to a shelf. 'There's a laptop over there if you wanna google it.'

I get up. 'You think I could find that sorta thing online?'

She smirks. 'Everything's online. Like, I'm guessing there'd at least be a news article, you know.'

I take the laptop from the shelf, sit back on the chaise lounge, and begin. Several search results reveal an endless list of news links to articles. After checking the top few, I realise I need to narrow my search by specifying Angel's full name and her as a victim of a car crash last December. This time, the search results reveal only a few. I click on the top link. And there she is, Angel, with her name and picture right at the top alongside another photo of a young guy. Immediately, I know that's him. *That's the kid who had his hands around her neck…*and his name—*Kurtis Neff.* I keep reading… *Wait?* Says he died on-site trying to save Angel. *What?* My mind fogs, confused, and I scowl. *That can't be right.* I close my eyes and try to remember that night, and it's the same, nothing more, not a goddamn thing. I scoff, annoyed. 'Bullshit!' I grunt. *He wasn't tryin' to help us.* There's no way I got this wrong, but now I've learned that he died that night too.

Candy checks in on me, but I ignore her, lost in the article. There's a mention of Kurt's wife at the crash site: Eleanor Neff. It paints her as a victim of losing her heroic husband. That's gotta be the woman's voice I heard that night. *I wish I knew what she said. She was just standin' there, watchin'. Did she want Angel dead?* I shut my eyes, frustrated, trying to remember, but I can't see anything more—just the same visions flash between my shattered mind, fighting to stay conscious.

I type in new searches, with Eleanor's full name—scanning articles, social media, maps, anything to find out where this woman could be. But it's hopeless. There's nothing. Clicking on "images", I scroll and scroll, but it feels hopeless. I glance away, frustrated, and catch Candy watching me. She looks back down at her tarot cards.

Just as I close the lid on the laptop, a small, obscure picture of Kurt with his arms around a girl catches my eye. I'm taken aback by how pretty she is. It looks like an old high school photo from a yearbook, scanned and uploaded. I click on it to get a better look, but the link is broken. It only seems to appear in the search results. *Is that her? Is that Eleanor in Kurt's arms?*

'You're gonna hurt them, aren't you?' Candy asks, catching me off guard, standing behind me, trepidation in her voice.

I let the silence sit for a moment as I look at her. 'Somethin' like that.'

Silence.

'Can I give you a reading?' she eventually asks.

I don't have to think long about answering this. 'I don't think that stuff's for me, Candy. The last thing I need to hear is some vague horoscope tellin' me how opportunities are just around the corner.'

She rolls her eyes. 'It's not like that! It's about…exploring your unconscious self.'

My unconscious self raises an eyebrow.

'Look, all you have to do is sit across from me. I don't even have to tell you what I read… please?'

This is how Angel was different. Things of the spiritual kind, the "Universe" or "God", seemed to reveal themselves to her. She didn't need all the toys and trinkets. It came naturally to her, less of a persona and more of an intuition—a way of life.

I give in to Candy's plea, offering, 'Okay,' at least it'll be an amusing distraction from the constant hollow feeling in my chest.

Night falls beneath candlelight. She sits back at her table and gently adjusts the tarot cards in an order that makes sense. Her demeanour shifts, and the mood in the room changes. I can feel the atmosphere of the air around me get heavier.

I take a seat at her little foldout table. She gathers her cards and shuffles them with care and affection like she's creating a physical connection with them. She pauses, holding the deck in her hand, and closes her eyes, as if praying. Opening her eyes, she looks at me and draws the first card. Pictured on that card is a naked woman wrapped in a cloth inside a large laurel wreath. She has one leg crossed over the other as if dancing. The naked woman is looking to one side, while her body moves forward in the opposite direction. In her hands are two wands, maybe batons, like the one a magician might have. Four figures are also on each corner of the card: a lion, a bull, a cherub, and an eagle.

She glances up at me. 'This card is the "World", but it's reversed.'

I don't know what any of that means. I meet her eyes. They're intense and purposeful.

'Do you want to know?' she asks.

I shrug. 'Sure, why not.'

'Well, honestly, I'm kinda not surprised by this one...' she opens a little leather-bound book that looks more like a journal, skimming several pages, and reads passages about the card's meaning. 'It has the meaning of missing something in your life...'

I smirk. *No shit.*

She continues, 'No closure... a feeling of incompletion; a cycle nearing its end, but not quite there. You're close, but something prevents you from seeing it. Both the world and these four heads on each corner speak to the cyclical nature of your life...'

My eyes drift to one side, past her, annoyed that I agreed to hear this shit.

'And... your progression through its cycles.'

I make a brief acknowledgement, and she draws the second card. On it are images of women, men, and children, depicted rising from caskets with their arms outspread, looking to the sky. Above them is an angel blowing a trumpet, and behind them all, in the background, is a massive tidal wave.

'Judgement,' she says.

I raise an eyebrow.

Tapping the card, her eyes meet mine again and she says, 'It's upright,' quickly searching her little book for its meaning. But I know what judgment means.

She confirms its meaning, reading out the words that stick out of the narrative echoing inside my head. Reckoning. Purging. And unavoidable judgment.

'The Judgement card reminds us we'll all face choices that'll have an astounding effect where your actions will change the course of your path, and there's no looking back. The consequences of those actions will eventually catch up to you...' She loses me when she suggests, 'all the pieces of the puzzle of your life are finally coming together to form one, unified picture of your life story.'

I adjust upright in my seat.

'Okay…' she says, 'last card. Future,' drawing the last card and placing it down gently.

A dog and a wolf stand in a grassy field, howling at a full moon in the night sky. They're positioned between two large towers and a path that leads off into the distance.

'The Moon…' she looks at me with trepidation and swallows, 'reversed,' her eyes drift slowly to nothing, as she considers it with a worrisome look, knowing its meaning… knowing something's not right.

She turns to her leather-bound book and flicks through a few pages, but I lay my hand on the page, covering it. 'Maybe we leave this one unsaid.'

She nods, slowly. 'Okay—I understand.'

I let go of her hand and walk across the room to the mini fridge to grab a beer. When I turn back around, twisting the cap off, she sits looking more concerned, lost in thought and holding the deck. She reads the pages anyway. I stare at her, swigging beer, wishing she hadn't. It's only now, having woken from an extended frozen state of darkness without a single dream, that I release what little life I was living, torn asunder by a couple of opportunistic kids. The cost was the death of an angel, my Angel. Closure, judgment… some bad hurt is coming. That's the decision I've already made. I didn't need a reading to know that. I've thought a thousand thoughts about living a more meaningful life, making it count and leaving something behind. But that's all any of it was… thoughts without action. Then Death finally came, and without warning, that son of a bitch didn't take me. He took my lover—my love, grinning at me with dead eyes inside a dead skull. And now, the thoughts I've had since waking have only been revenge, bloody, hurtful revenge. These are the puzzle pieces of my life. I'm a dog: restless, a wolf, lone and on the hunt. This is my meaning. This is what I'm making count and the something I'm leaving behind will be two corpses.

I lay back on the bed, tired, in a food coma, and I feel the impatience of my thoughts manifest themselves, churning in my chest. I know I need to stop thinking that I'm missing out, that I'm letting Angel down. I try to remember this didn't happen yesterday—that the crash was a year ago and that Angel is… I sit up.

'What is it?' Asks Candy.

'I'm ready now.'

THE LAST GOODBYE, SOMETHING ROMANTIC

19/12

Frank's different. He's lost his spark. My heart aches for him. It's been ages now and I don't know where he went or why. Something about going to get a bird? I dunno. Watching him stand over Angel's grave earlier was so surreal. I've always thought cemeteries were so creepy. Maybe that's just a me thing. I asked him if he wanted company, but he said he wanted to be alone. I get that.

I could've hurt him earlier, but I knew he was just letting me believe I could. I wouldn't of course. I'm just a stubborn bitch sometimes. He's the only guy in the universe I trust. Whatever he did to sway my family to have Oscar in my life again—I'd do anything for him. We could never be anything more than what we are, whatever that is. Wish I could've heard what he was saying to her. I imagine it's the last goodbye, something romantic.

Tonight's moon is enormous. I noticed it above
him earlier at her tombstone as I remembered the
last card I drew. I take it back. I don't wanna know
what he said to Angel.

I think it'd scare me.

SORRY TO HAVE BOTHERED YOU

I loiter in the laneway of my former apartment block, near the back entrance. Ducking down between dumpsters, I watch and wait for someone to exit. Thirty minutes or so pass before someone leaves and I can slide out, like a passing shadow. Moving swiftly and quietly between the closing doors, I enter. I walk through the underground car park toward the elevator. A car alarm echoes in the din, followed by clomping footsteps. I survey the lot and see a couple heading towards the elevator; they see me, so I keep my head down and feel my trouser pockets, making it appear like I've left my keys upstairs as we converge at the elevator.

We stand in the elevator. One woman tries to be polite by ignoring my appearance. The other woman, whom I initially thought was a man because of her stature, heavy denim jacket and face like a Rottweiler, presses the button to go up.

I come out on level five. The place doesn't appear to have changed much—*still drab*. The door to my old apartment is just down the hall.

I stand outside my old apartment door, *Lucky 13*, and reach up above the doorframe to where I used to keep my spare key. I feel the grime and dust along the edge and then cold metal—*it's still 'ere.* I step back, feeling the cut groves of the key with my thumb and recognise there's too much light in the hallway. Pocketing the key, I drag a ceramic pot with its fake plastic fern from the side of the wall to underneath a fluorescent lamp and use it to reach up and quickly remove the plastic light fixtures, exposing the fluorescent tube within. Gently twisting the tube, I loosen it and it blinks off. I place the plastic fixture back, push the fake fern back against the wall and approach my apartment door again, taking out the spare key. *Let's hope whoever's inside didn't do their due diligence and change the locks. I don't know what type of people live 'ere...I don't want to cause a scene, but it may be unavoidable.*

I slide the key into the keyhole and twist. The door unlocks. Gently, trying to make as little sound as possible, I open it, but the rusty hinges creak anyway—a sound I'd forgotten but quickly recognise. I should've known better. I hear the movement of kitchen chairs sliding back against wooden floorboards...*'ere we go.* I shove the door all the way open and turn quickly to my right, flicking off the light switch to the apartment. People stand alarmed, crowded around a table. It's a family—caught off guard. They must have been having a late-night meal. There's a mother and a father with two kids, a boy and a girl. They're Muslims: easily identified by the father's beard and the daughter's hijab. The mother is nervously caught, not wearing one. I must appear like a shadowy ghost to them, a thin tall silhouetted figure with square shoulders thanks to the old blokes's tweed coat. I place my left hand in my jacket pocket, pretending to wield a pistol and step forward into the dim light from a small lamp beside a television. Frightened, the mother quickly embraces her children and, speaking Arabic I assume, she tells them to get behind her. They do. She shouts at me too, scared out of her wits. The father is equally rattled and yells at me and then at his wife, which I'm guessing is to calm her down—for her to be quiet.

'SHUT UP!' I coarsely growl.

Startled, they quiet. The mother tries to silence her terrified, whimpering children by clasping her hands around their mouths. We all stare at each other silently for a moment. I close the door behind me.

The father calmly pleads with broken English, 'Please—don't hurt my babies. Who are you? What do you want?'

These are the usual ramblings a terrified man asks for his family's safety, the kind of stuff that doesn't matter and gets in the way.

Glaring at him I slowly growl. 'I said shut up.'

The father does as he's told. I step closer. The mother retreats with her children and the father steps between us.

I raise a hand. 'I'm not 'ere for you. I won't hurt you. I just need to get somethin' from the bedroom.'

He stares at me, confusion clouding his dark eyes. 'From bedroom? What you need?'

I reiterate, 'I said, shut up.'

I point to his wife and kids. 'Lock 'em in the bathroom.'

They stare at me, too afraid to move.

'Now—move!' I shout gruffly, pointing to the bathroom.

The father hustles his frightened family inside, instructing them around the corner to the bathroom, assuring their safety. I follow, my hand pointed in the old bloke's coat pocket. The father closes the bathroom door with his family anxiously cuddled inside and, in Arabic, tells them, I assume, to lock the door.

I hear the bathroom lock click and shift my attention to the father. 'Go to the bedroom.'

Inside I tell him, 'Lay on the floor. Spread your arms wide. Face the wall away from me.'

He does as he's told again. I move to the built-in wardrobe, slide the mirrored door open and crouch. Removing several stacked dusty shoe boxes from the inside, I place them on the bed behind me and lean forward, reaching in, feeling the back of the floor for a pinky-sized hole. I find it and use my pinky finger to lift a floorboard out, revealing a hidden space underneath. Reaching down, I feel inside. *Thank*

Christ, it's still 'ere. I remove an old red fishing tackle box and place it at my feet. Looking over at the father, I can see he's still facing away from me. I stare at him momentarily, listening to him breathe. Opening the red tackle box, I remove the plastic compartment divider, and there she is. *Caged up for too long.* I reach inside, and take out my Tweety Bird: a .45 automatic Colt pistol with the grip tightly masked with a few layers of yellow electric tape—I simply like the feel of it. Also inside is a box of .45 cartridges alongside some cash: a mix of "pineapples" and twenties folded and bound by a red elastic band. I pocket the money in the old bloke's coat and shuffle the box of cartridges into the left coat pocket. I pause, knowing it'd be here and that if I saw it, it might break me. But I had no choice. I needed my Tweety.

Sitting back on my ass, I rest the tackle box over my crossed legs and stare at it momentarily, unsure if I should even touch it, let alone bring it. I reach inside and take out a classic white disposable BIC cigarette lighter. I spark her. She still works. I close my eyes and clench my fist around the lighter. Aside from my memories of Angel, which feel like they're slowly fading, this is the only thing of hers I have left. I glance to my right. Fearless but sorrowful, the father stares at me as if into my soul. I've let my guard down.

'Stop lookin' at me.' I spit, picking up Tweety and aiming.

He doesn't flinch. Instead, he offers me an invitation, 'Please, eat with me.'

I glare at him. 'What?'

He sits up, showing the palms of his hands, 'Eat with me. Please.'

I sit frozen with Tweety aimed. The father stands and gestures for me to follow him as he exits the bedroom without fear of being hurt. I'm unsure why or how, but the situation's dynamic has shifted. I hear the bathroom door unlock. I hear the father speak, calming his anxious wife. Footsteps patter. I get to my feet and walk out of the bedroom.

The family sits nervously around their table in the living

room, Tweety aimed at them. The father gestures towards an empty chair.

'Please, sit.'

I feel oddly calm, as if under a spell or a prayer. I lower Tweety and take a seat at their table. The father nods at his wife and she sighs back at him. I can tell she's uncomfortable and doesn't want me here, especially with Tweety around her children, but she serves me food from their platters anyway. One kid stares at Tweety, so I hide her, shoving her between the seat cushion and my thigh. The father looks to his family with an assuring smile, eventually landing his smile on me.

I look down at the large plate of food in front of me: lamb skewers with a healthy dollop of Baba ghanoush, alongside kibbeh and tabbouleh. It smells good, but I'm unfamiliar with the other food on my dish.

'What's this one?' I ask.

'Tashreeb Dajaj,' replies the father, gesturing for me to try it.

Using a fork, I skewer what looks like chicken and take a bite. It tastes incredible, and that's an understatement. I nod, thanking them as I chew, holding back tears.

Silently, we eat. I can see the father's mind at work, wanting to tell me something. His eyes stare towards the table of food, and his lips twitch. Maybe he's thinking about how to word whatever he feels I need to hear. The family pauses. I place my fork beside my plate, and the father looks over at me.

'Your eyes. They used to be my eyes.'

'How's that?' I ask him.

'Pain. Anger…I had these eyes…in the corners,' pointing to his own, 'Is where the fear hides, scared.' He says again, 'I had these eyes.' He stands up and lifts his shirt revealing burn scars across his belly and back. 'From war, fighting Taliban.' His wife shuffles in her seat, her face disapproves, and she looks to her children and gestures not to stare. He tucks his

shirt in and sits back down. 'But I escape. Marry, have children. Inshallah, my eyes change.'

I know what he's getting at, find a nice woman and settle
down, have a family and god willing the pain goes away.
Naive advice if you ask me. He doesn't know me or what's
going on—only knows what he knows and what worked for
him. I wouldn't doubt for a second that he's probably seen
some horrible shit go down, even likely by his own hands.
Although I can't speak too much on the horrors of modern
warfare, I know that in face-to-face combat, it's either you or
them, kill or be killed... No, my war story is a little different.
Although I am curious, I'm afraid to learn more—to ask
where he was stationed, afraid to find out that we may have
crossed paths, with each side believing they're fighting the
good fight. That's what we were told—made to believe. Even
a box-filling dead-shit like me—every bit counts, everyone
matters. Lies. I don't feel much like swapping war stories.
Mine's a can of worms. I guess we were meant to cross paths
anyway…anyway. Good for him and his. I look around at my
old apartment. *I don't belong 'ere.*

'I used to live 'ere.' I tell them.

I pocket Tweety in the old bloke's coat and stand. 'I don't
belong 'ere anymore. Sorry to have bothered you.'

Just as I'm about to leave, I see a pair of old Reeboks. I
bend down and size them against my foot. They're a good fit,
perfect even. I turn to the family and take in the home they've
made for themselves. Although it's clean and homely, it needs
work and knowing the landlords, nothing will get done. But
they've made it work. I take my five-hundred-dollar bundle
of cash and toss it to the father. 'For the shoes,' I tell him, as I
leave their apartment for the first; mine for the last time.

* * *

Time feels as if it's passing quickly—an intuitive sense of
danger rings alarms in the back of my mind. I keep off the

main streets, passing through the city again, back on foot, but not literally this time. I'm walking on clouds with these Reeboks. They were worth the money.

I stop at the sight of red and blue lights, and they silently flash ahead of me. I can't tell if they're police or ambos. I'm unsure if anyone would be on the lookout for me since having escaped the hospital a few weeks back.

No one turned up to the Drum asking. And I can't say I trust the Muslim family, even if they did feed me; the $500 may not have covered the trauma. Maybe they called the police after I left. Can't risk passing the red and blue. Ahead of me is a laneway to my left, and I take it.

I must be in some semi-industrial neighbourhood, factory lots, warehouses, cheap apartments, roller doors, wheelie bins and commercial dumpsters. I see the silhouette of a stray cat walking a fence line. It halts, spooked, watching me as I pass.

Without warning, I'm pushed in the back and tripped, falling face-first onto cobbled stones. I see blood and feel pain shoot through my skull from the point of my chin to my crown. *That's all I need—more facial scarrin'.*

Light shifts, and from out of the shadows, several silhou-etted figures surround me. I try to spin and get up, but a knee from one of them hits me in the back while another knee presses against my neck. *Trouble finds me.*

'You see this motherfucker's face? It's all, like, scarred and shit. Like that scissor-hands, dude.' That's the first voice I hear. Male, twenties. Speaks fast, almost paranoid.

'Nah man, fuck'n Freddy Krueger,' laughter from a second voice, also male, twenties and with an anxious pace.

'One…two…Freddy's com-in for you,' that's the first voice again, and he's off-tune.

'Hold his ass down while I grab his wallet,' a third voice, another male, could be in his early thirties. He speaks with a little more control. This one's the alpha.

He frisks me, not knowing what he's feeling in the old bloke's left coat pocket. He struggles to release it and wrenches the box of cartridges, tearing the pocket. That pisses me off.

'What is it?' The second one asks.

'Fuck me,' says the alpha, 'Keep holding him.'

He searches me again and finds Tweety inside.

'Shit! He's a fucking cop!' shouts the first one, scared they've fucked up.

'He's not a cop!' the alpha shouts back, 'and keep your fucking voice down!'

'He got a wallet, badge?' I hear the second one ask.

The Alpha searches for more but only finds the white cigarette lighter. He tosses it away, and that really pisses me off.

'He's not a cop,' declares the alpha, kicking me in the ribs. 'What are ya?'

I take the pain and keep my mouth shut. I got no idea what these guys look like and whether I stand a chance—*still, it could be fun.* He smacks the back of my head as if that'll woo me to speak. I remain silent.

'Ah—fuck this guy! Asshole ain't got shit anyway,' says the second one.

They turn me over, keeping me pinned. I get a good look at each of them. One doesn't look too dissimilar to how I looked in the hospital: gaunt with sores and bad facial hair. But this guy's stringy and greasy; he looks like a rat. Two is also gaunt, but with no facial hair and a bald, tattooed head, he looks like a snake. The alpha has a little meat on the bone, short hair, facial stubble surrounding craters of acne scars and fresh blisters. He looks like a diseased mutt. Each has scratches up and down on their forearms, and their eyes are fully dilated. *Junkies.* Without knowing what they're fuelled by, ice, meth or some other new street drug manufactured in some backyard garage, cut with god knows what, I need to be careful. That's what makes junkies dangerous and unpredictable, and any little thing could set them off. *I hate junkies. Got no time or sympathy.*

'He's a fucking junkie!' says the rat.

The irony. I crack up, laughing.

'He's fucked! Let's have some fun,' says the alpha mutt.

'Yeah, fuck this guy up!' shouts the snake.

I grit my teeth, grinning. *I like this idea.*

Snake and rat lift me to my feet, keeping my arms pinned behind me. The alpha mutt takes Tweety and aims her at me, but I know this Mutt's all bark, no bite. He's trying to scare me, but I don't scare easily. I've been through the worst of it now.

I keep smiling. The alpha mutt looks around nervously, second-guessing. He knows the noise he'll bring if he makes Tweety chirp. He lowers her and looks at the other two behind me. He's fidgety and I'm pissed off, beginning to get bored.

Tensing up, I stomp on the foot of the rat to my right, my arm loosening from his grip, and I drive my elbow sharply into his temple. He drops, sleeping stiffly. Before he can aim Tweety, I follow up by kicking alpha mutt in the groin; he crumbles to his knees, crying. I spin, twisting the snake's arm to use as leverage, following up with a clean right hook to his fragile jaw, shattering it. Wrestling Tweety from the mutt's grip, I have myself some fun for the next several minutes!

I make a bloody mess as I beat on each of them, pistol-whipping them with bone-cracking aggression and teeth-clenching kicks. Even in my broken state these junkie fucks never stood a chance. I wipe sweat from my brow, leaving a smear of blood, like war paint. I stand hunched over, brooding, Tweety in hand. Staring down the void of darkness at one end of the laneway, my knuckles drip with blood and my breaths are deep and long. A resurrection of violent intentions has risen from a birthing pool, proving to me I'm born again. I'm ready.

My box of cartridges is broken and empty. I feel around and pick up as many as I can see and pocket them in my pants. I find the white lighter underneath a dumpster and clean it with my shirt, sparking it. It's still good. I place it back inside the old bloke's coat pocket, near my heart. Red and blue lights silently flash once again. I gather myself, ensuring I have all I need, and dash into the next street. Then, running several blocks on adrenaline alone, I reach the closest train station.

* * *

Back at the Drum, inside Candy's room, I sit gazing at nothing with half a beer as she attends to my fresh wounds with Mederma and a wet cloth, dabbing at the new facial scarring on my chin.

'You should've just let me take you there and back.'

'Maybe... just feelin' cooped up in 'ere is all. Need to stretch my legs.'

Speaking of, I get up, finish the beer and toss it in a nearby bin. She restocked the mini-fridge and got Crown larger for some reason. I always preferred Pilsners. So did Angel.

I grab another gold-wrapped bottle and stare towards nothing, taking a swig. 'Didn't think they made Crownies anymore.'

'Client's request.' She tells me.

'Wanker,' I chuff, 'what is he, a cop?'

She looks away, ashamed to admit it.

I pause, bothered, and then it occurs to me... I bail up to her and ask, 'It's not O'Leary, is it?'

She hesitates, but eventually nods.

'What the fuck, Candice!' I shout, using her real name for the first time in a long time, 'I thought that piece of shit was banned from 'ere?'

'He was!' she replies, agitatedly, 'but things have changed. He's allowed now.'

'That fuck beat on you girls—he beat on you bad, Candice!' that's twice now that I've caught myself using her real name, 'you remember that! Black and blue you were!

You couldn't work for months. Angel had to pay your share.'

She stands, throwing her hands down. 'I know that! I don't need you to fucking remind me of that, okay!' Flustered, she moves to the window. 'I don't have a choice. I need the money. I got a little boy, you know…'

Shaken and shaking, she cries, 'You don't think I want out of here—to be with Oscar?' The black eyeliner she must've only just retouched runs down her cheeks.

I storm out of the room and march downstairs, finding Madame Lacey in the lobby greeting some asshole in a suit. I bail up, grab her by the arm and pull her behind closed doors.

'What the hell do you think you're doing—get your hands off me!' she snaps.

I shove her against the wall.

Nicky jumps in, trying to hold me back, pleading. 'Shit Frank! Don't do anything stupid!'

I ignore him, glaring through Madame Lacey. 'All that shit about this place being good for the girls, and yet you allow that fuck O'Leary back in 'ere?'

She glares right back, daggers in her bright blue eyes. 'You don't know what you're talking about.'

'No!?'

'You don't understand—let me go!' she growls, trying to pull away.

But I shove her back. *I'm not finished.* 'Make me understand why you allow that cunt to be alone with the girls!'

'He's not alone with them.'

'How else would you put it then, mum?…just Candice then?'

She stops trying to leave, taking a breath. 'For fuck's sake, you are so dramatic,' straightening her dress and posture, daggers still in her eyes, 'I had to sacrifice one for the many… I'm sorry. I hate it, but here we are. O'Leary's the reason this place stays open now… okay.'

She slinks away from me.

'It's okay,' Nicky quietly tells me, as he pats my shoulder.

I brush him off like lint. 'The fuck it is.'

Madame Lacey pauses at the door and peers back over her shoulder. 'Don't ever fucking touch me again.'

I saunter back to Candy's room. She's still crying at the window.

I try to comfort her. 'I'm sorry. I wasn't judgin' you... I just....' I hug her, staring at nothing. A thought crosses my mind, an idea, one of high risk, but I put it away.

* * *

It's the following day. I'm lying on the chaise lounge, and I haven't slept. The high-risk idea has infested my mind, playing out repeatedly and in different ways, countering all that could be wrong with it.

'Frank, you up?' asks Candy from her bed, closing her journal.

I put the thought away.

* * *

It's three in the afternoon. I can't shake this risky idea from my mind. I keep seeing it play out with success. Pacing around the room, the idea both excites and scares me. I pause, staring at Candy sitting on the fire escape outside the window, reading. It occurs to me—*I'm a hypocrite.*

* * *

Near dinner time Candy snaps, annoyed, 'Just what? What is it? You've been weird all day! Pacing around, slumped on the chaise lounge, staring at empty space. You've barely said a word to me since last night. But then you'll be looking at me with some weird look. It's like you're here, but you're not here, and it annoys me. What is it? Do you need to get out or something? Like, what, what is it?'

I sit up on the chaise lounge.

'You're right, I'm sorry.' But I turn away. I still can't bring myself to tell her—to ask her.

She tilts her head. 'Frank…C'mon.'

Leaning back, I spill, 'I think we can help each other out… but I don't feel good about it. It's high risk—dangerous,' I walk over to her, 'a lot of girls say they want out, Candy, but they don't. A lot of girls get out but don't stay out. So…I need to hear from you. Cause there won't be any comin' back with what I'm about to ask of you. Candice, do you want out?'

She stares at me, seemingly intrigued. 'Go on…'

'I reckon we can kill two birds with one stone, hell— maybe three.'

* * *

I extend the legs of an Inca-branded tripod; it's flimsy but it'll do. Candy hands me a camcorder, a Canon MV500 that's seen better days. It's dirty and needs to be powered by a wall adapter because its battery no longer charges. I fix it on the tripod, position it out of sight, hidden within a wardrobe and run its power cable from a point in the bathroom. I scatter clothes, making a mess along the cable to hide it. She keeps an untidy room anyway.

She fidgets with her hair next to me. 'I'm worried about this, Frank.'

'I know, me too, but don't be. It'll work.'

'It's not that. I mean, what if the tape gets lost or finds its way online? I know what I do holds shame, but at least it's not a public shame for all the world to see… and for Oscar to see, you know?'

'It won't.'

I place the tape into the camcorder and press record, telling her to get on the bed. I direct her to move into different positions that she knows O'Leary has an appetite for.

Opening the closet door, I stop recording. 'Should be enough now to play back with.'

I rewind the tape and play it back, flipping out the camcorder's little LCD screen and watch the footage.

Seeing Candy on screen and hearing my voice through the tiny, tinny-sounding camcorder speakers, directing her, I feel like a pornographer. *I don't like this.* It's the part I knew I wouldn't. I couldn't see it a few minutes ago, but now I can, captured in 720p; she's uncomfortable. I don't feel right. I press stop and turn to her. She's seated in the middle of the bed, biting her nails and looking at me.

I sigh, 'I'm sorry. You don't have to do this. I'll find another way.'

'No—it's okay. It has to be this way,' she says, unbuttoning her shirt, but leaving her bra on, 'things have been quiet for me...I'm not getting as many requests as I did. It's how O'Leary wanted it.'

I look at her puzzled. 'What do you mean? You're one of Madame Lacey's best earners?'

She slowly removes her bra, revealing what that sick fuck O'Leary did to her. My eyes trail down to where her left nipple should have been. Instead, there's just a nasty scar.

I look up from her scarred breast and into her eyes. We hold a stare. I don't know what to say, so I say nothing, anger swelling deep in my belly.

'I probably shouldn't say this, but...' she looks away, thinking if she should continue or not, but I know she will.

I already know what she's about to say, so I let her say it because I know she needs to. 'I just wanted to let you know that... if, maybe you ever wanted to, if you could, be with someone again or—I don't know what I'm saying...'

My anger ebbs away, and I join her on the bed. I kiss her

chest, right where her heart is. I kiss her scar and then her neck. I run my hand along the right side of her cheek and kiss her lips gently. I'm ashamed to admit how much I need to feel this—a human connection. I know Angel will understand.

Candy removes my shirt and together we make each other feel like we're the only people in the world worth loving.

* * *

Later, looking through the LCD flip screen, I adjust the camcorder frame, zooming in on Candy. She's dressed like a Geisha in a floral-patterned kimono a Shimada wig, intense black winged eye makeup and lush red lipstick. That asshole O'Leary is feeling like Japanese tonight. I try not to think about all the things I want to do to him for what he's done to her, but I push those feelings away—concentrate on the mission.

'Alright…I'm ready,' she turns to tell me.

I look up from behind the camera and nod. She leaves to fetch O'Leary who's waiting downstairs in the lobby. I hit the record button on the camcorder and close the wardrobe door. It's hidden, but I leave a slim enough gap for the camera to see through.

I hide in the bathroom where I'll be staked out. It's a bit cold in here, so I put on the old bloke's coat. Tweety's in the pocket. I wait. Staring at tiny smatters of black mould along the edges of the white tiles and cracks in the grout fixed around the bathtub, I marvel at how, even with the elements of moisture and condensation working against them, the tiles still hold on.

I hear the door open and sit up, staring at the back of the bathroom door. I pay close attention, listening carefully to every sound. I hear them enter the room and the door close. I listen to them speak. She's in character, speaking the little Japanese she knows. O'Leary sounds too drunk to even care, and I doubt he would, even if the prick was sober.

74

She moves things forward. I hear a zipper unzipping and the ruffling of clothes undressing. She's touching him. She wants this to be over quickly and so do I. I want to distract my mind from having to listen to the two of them, but I can't. I have to hear him say the most horrid shit. *I hate this fuck.*

'Slow down, bitch!' O'Leary shouts.

Careful Candy. Just get through it like you always do. You won't ever have to—SLAP!

O'Leary snaps. 'I said to slow down! Stupid fucking cunt!'

Jumping to my feet, scowling, I clench my fists. *He hit her! That son of bitch hit her!*

'Sumimasen, sempai,' she cries, continuing.

What've I done…I've become my father.

I pause listening. Their movement sounds aggressive. She whimpers, hurt, and I'm unsure if this is part of the role-play or if she's actually in pain—*Damnit! We should've come up with some sort of safe word or sound, just somethin' for me to know if things get dicey.*

The sound of O'Leary's hoarse rasp is unsettling. I pace in tight circles within the two-meter space of her tiny en suite, and then I catch my reflection in the mirror, my brow beading with sweat. Listening to the depraved guttural drawl from a guy whose teeth I want to smash in while he gets off is grating…*I need to stay focused.* It sounds like it's coming to an end anyway.

'Ouch! What're you doing?' she complains.

I spin towards the door. She sounds upset. I listen attentively. They seemed to have stopped. I hear footsteps.

'Where're you going?' she asks.

Each of O'Leary's staggered steps sound closer. He's approaching the bathroom. I take Tweety out of the old bloke's coat pocket and hold out, inching closer to the door.

'What is this?' O'Leary asks. He sounds close.

I wipe the sweat from my brow, press Tweety against the door, listening and aim, ready. I gently pull back on Tweety's tail.

'Is there another rooster in the hen house?' O'Leary demands. *Fuck!*

'What? No—that's just…old clothes… I was cleaning out my wardrobe earlier…' she refutes, 'and—no!—don't open that!'

I hear the wardrobe door creek open.

'What the fuck!?' hawks O'Leary.

Shit!—The camera! I swing the door open, and with Tweety aimed at his head, I pounce on him like Sylvester. Startled, looking confused and half-naked, he quickly turns and tries for his holstered revolver hanging from his belt, looped around the bedpost. But I catch him, quickly switching Tweety to safety, then whipping her across his pretty face, busting open a bloody gash. He drops hard, groaning, hurt. Blood gushes from his sharp nose. The sudden violence rattles Candy and she shivers fearfully against the bedhead. I feel much better, looking down at O'Leary's bloody face.

'My fucking nose!' he shouts.

I stand over him as he gets to one knee, cupping his hand over his bloody face. He looks up, staring down Tweety's barrel. I flick the safety off and cock her tail. This blue-eyed piece of shit looks past Tweety and into my eyes.

He drops his hand, staring at me and sneers, 'I know you.'

I punch him hard in the face, sending his defined jawline in the opposite direction. He slumps to the floor, out cold. I pocket Tweety and turn to Candy.

'He's sleepin',' I say, reaching down to lift his legs. 'C'mon, give me a hand.'

* * *

As it turns out, O'Leary's now the Chief Superintendent. He's also a family man with two kids and a wife, regularly attending Sunday services and charity events for cripples and seniors. He's also a scumbag who solicits and beats up working girls to make himself feel like a big man. O'Leary's still passed out, half-naked and tied to a chair in Candy's bathroom. I stand across from him, holding Tweety and a mini DV videotape with incriminating footage in one hand. Candy sits on the lip of her bathtub, biting her nails. Her black-winged eye makeup remains while she changes out of the kimono and wig.

O'Leary comes to. I aim Tweety at him. He's groggy and dazed. Groaning, he looks up at me and around the room. His head must be spinning. He shifts his focus to Candy, gazing at her. His eyes light up and he jerks suddenly, trying to stand but realises he's tied to a chair.

'What is this shit!' he barks, scowling with an unsettling glare at her, 'you're finished. This whole fucking place is finished. I'm going to burn this—'

I cock Tweety's tail, gaining his attention. He shuts up.

I hold up the videotape. 'You can guess what's on this?'

He spits out blood on the rug. 'Yeah, I can guess. Fuck do you want?'

'Information. Names and addresses.'

'What the fuck are you talking about—you want information?' he snarls, spitefully.

'Shut up and listen!' I bark back.

Candy looks to the floor, worried this isn't working.

'There was a crash almost a year back. I need the couple's names who were involved, the witnesses at the scene, and I need to know where they are,' I sternly reiterate.

O'Leary looks at me curiously with his beady little blood-shot blue eyes; somehow, they seem as dark as mine. 'How do I know you? I've seen you before...'

Candy glances nervously at me.

I get up close to O'Leary, shoving the videotape in his face. 'Everyone's gonna know you if we put this tape out. Your life won't be worth spit! Got it!'

He turns, glaring at Candy. 'Yeah. I get it.'

'You look at me!' I bark.

He turns his eyes back on me. 'You haven't given me

much to go on. It may take some time to find the information you're after.'

I scribble the details of what I need to know on a piece of scrap paper and shove it in his mouth. 'Then ya better get started.'

CAN OF WORMS

Candy and I sit across from each other on red, worn pleather seats in the back of a pizzeria. Our teenage waitress makes her way towards our booth with a Margherita pizza. It's a decent place with a Manhattan diner aesthetic. Patrons chat away to the backdrop of clinking cutlery and a humming espresso machine. There's a couple of long-haired forty-year-olds wearing flannel shirts in the kitchen, cooking while singing along to *Monkey Gone to Heaven* by the Pixies, which plays throughout the pizzeria. My kinda place if I had known about it. The teenage waitress drops off our pizza with a forced smile. *Melted cheese and oregano never smelt so good.*

Candy sprinkles chilli flakes across it. 'You don't mind, do you?'

'Course not.' I reply.

It's been a couple of hours since we cut O'Leary loose. But he contacted us about forty-five minutes ago, telling me he had what I wanted and for us to meet him here. I wasn't sure why he chose this place until we drove past earlier and saw a police station just around the corner. Chewing a mouthful of pizza, Candy pops her head out from the booth.

She gulps, gesturing towards the entrance. 'He's here,' she says sliding out from her seat, joining me.

I turn and see the square-jawed pretty boy at the entrance. Keeping a low profile, he glances at his wristwatch, sees us and makes his way along the row of booths, taking a seat opposite.

I warned Candy earlier that she needed to relax when he arrived. I explained how she'd play her part. We act like we're all friends, hanging out, shooting the shit and eating pizza. But I don't take my own advice, seething with cold, intense, anger—making O'Leary uncomfortable. He's twitchy and on edge. I imagine doing some hurtful things to his smug face. She notices and nudges me with her elbow and I snap out of it.

His mouth curls into a smirk, his dull blue eyes glistening with arrogance. 'Frank Conway…yeah, you were famous for a while there, weren't you? Sorry, infamous. A drug-mule in the army.'

Candy pauses mid-bite on a slice and glances at me, but I stay quiet and steadfast, still seething.

He places a half-inch thick manila folder filled with paper on the table, keeping his left hand on top while lowering his right hand underneath. 'What, too soon?… I knew I knew you. It's funny how we've never run into each other before— quite bizarre, actually.'

I force a smile. 'Is that everythin' I asked for?'

'My oath—made for very interesting reading, Frank,' he offers, 'terrible accident and all,' he finishes with mock sympathy.

I don't bite and let Candy do her part. She reaches into her handbag and removes the videotape, placing it on the table and resting her hand on it.

'Are there copies?' O'Leary asks, cocking an eyebrow at me.

'We wouldn't have time to do that!' she snaps.

Without looking at her, he spits, 'Shut ya fucking slut mouth. I'm talking to him.'

'Cock sucker!' she fires back.

He chuckles, slowly turning to her. 'Nah baby, that's you.'

She pounces to slap him, but I pull her back to the seat.

O'Leary's attention turns back to me. 'Good man, keep your fucking dog on a leash.'

I hold my icy glare.

He reaches for the tape, but Candy slides it back towards herself.

'Folder first,' I demand.

I hear the sound of a gun cock from underneath the table.

'Heh,' murmurs O'Leary, his mouth breaking into a grin, 'is my gun pointed at you or at her?' He shakes his head. 'Give me the tape, and I'll hand you the folder.'

I don't budge. She adjusts, nudging forward in her seat, releasing her left hand from over the tape to meet her right underneath the table. O'Leary looks down between his legs, then quickly back up at her. Together, we watch his cocky expression shift to dread. She smirks. He has the barrel of a sawed-off shotgun uncomfortably positioned and aimed at his balls. I take Tweety from the old bloke's coat, place her on the table with my left hand and slide the oversized three-fold laminate menu over her with my right, pulling back on her tail, ready to fire. A bead of sweat rolls down his brow. He breaks eye contact with me, glancing at Candy, then looks back down between his crotch. He quaffs whatever saliva he'd built up in his mouth and looks back at me again.

'Slowly.' I tell him, pointing to the menu.

He removes his pistol from underneath the table and slides it under the menu, slowly. I snatch it, pocketing it in the old bloke's coat.

'Now the folder.'

He does so reluctantly. I open it and scan through the papers. I come to a photograph and it's surreal: my old car but a complete wreck on the edge of a riverbank held by a cable truck.

Looking over my shoulder, Candy gasps, 'Jeez... How'd

you even survive that?' alarmed by the graphic image of the car wreck.

I turn a page, and there's a morgue photograph of Angel—all life and spirit drained from her, cold and sickly blue. I wish I hadn't seen it. Candy looks away. The image is too much for her. I shut my eyes and try to remember the Polaroid in Candy's room, the one of Angel smiling. I turn to the next page, opening my eyes: There's another profile with another morgue image. It's the kid: Kurt. I can feel Candy looking at me, concerned. I glance at her crooked, and she understands. She turns her attention back on O'Leary and adjusts the shotgun barrel between his legs.

'Are we done here?' he asks restlessly, glancing at his wristwatch, sweat stains under his armpits.

Annoyed by his distraction, I slam my fist on the table. The cutlery rattles, and the salt and pepper shakers tip over. He keeps quiet with nervous tension. Several patrons turn and look up toward us.

Candy looks at each of them with a "Can I help you?" smile, and they return to their meals.

My finger runs along the text as I read the report, trying to understand more about what happened.

It confirms what I read online, Kurt had drowned while trying to help, caught inside the wreck, which threw the car—my car, off balance, causing it to tip into a ravine.

I keep reading and learn more about Eleanor—transcript: *"...we saw a car crashed off the side of the highway. We pulled over and went to help... we saw the car crashed against a tree... Kurt called triple zero... I remember looking at the car, thinking how dangerously unstable it was... I told Kurt to be careful, but he wanted to help anyway..."*

There's no way I have this wrong. 'This is garbage!'

O'Leary and Candy remain awkwardly silent.

I take the photo of her from underneath the transcript and I'm taken aback. She kinda looks like Angel. *I gotta find this girl, Eleanor, and make her admit it, make her say that they wanted us dead. Make her tell me the truth!*

I turn a page to clippings held with a paperclip and run my fingers along more text to Eleanor's last known address.

'Accordin' to this, she lives down the south coast,' I mutter, lifting the page out and folding it, placing it within the old bloke's coat. 'Let's go!'

Candy carefully pulls the shotgun barrel out from between O'Leary's crotch and hides it back in a duffle bag underneath our seat.

'Hey! What about the tape?' exclaims O'Leary.

Candy blows O'Leary a kiss, waving goodbye with her pinky finger, probably the same one she used to peg him with. She slides out and leaves the pizzeria, carrying the duffle bag. O'Leary reaches for the tape, and I fuck with him again, removing the menu and leaning over the table, digging Tweety's beak into his chest.

'Hey, hey—hey! We had a deal!' he demands, panicked, his hands raised, as he looks to see if anyone else can see us.

'I'm addin' a new condition,' I tell him through gritted teeth, 'you're never to see her again. You never touch her—you never think about her—nothin'. Got it!'

He nods. 'Yeah, whatever—couldn't give a fuck about that whore anyway, mate.'

I settle and sit back.

'So are we done here?'

I nod, pocketing Tweety and get out from behind the booth. As I turn to leave, O'Leary grabs the mini videotape and I catch him rechecking his wristwatch, but I think nothing of it. As I make my way through the restaurant, two uniformed officers enter ahead of me at the entrance; they look past me, back over my shoulder. O'Leary's smirking. I look back at the officers ahead of me and their eyes are now on me, with their hands moving towards their holsters.

'GUN!' I hear O'Leary shout.

The two officers immediately draw their pistols, shouting, 'On the ground!'

Shock hits the staff and patrons freeze, confused. It happens quickly—a twitch reflex and I sidestep behind a nearby waiter, using him as a shield. I draw Tweety and fire at the officers at close range. Each round tears through their chests, bursting holes out through their backs. The shop front glass shatters behind them. The gunfire is deafening and the flash of fire Tweety spits is startling to everyone but me. At the same time, I toss the waiter down and the officers collapse to the floor. Staff and patrons scream, frightened, and duck under tables while others freeze. Candy screeches to a halt in her car, pulling up on the street outside, and in the commotion, I dash out of the pizzeria's entrance.

The passenger door to her car flings open, and I dive in. Frazzled, Candy jams the gearshift into "neutral" by accident, the motor revving uselessly. I scramble, sitting up, and see O'Leary out the passenger window. Inside the pizzeria, he's crouched beside the wounded officers and looks up at me with vengeful eyes. He reaches quickly for one of the officer's pistols and aims it at us, but I'm suddenly hauled back in the passenger seat, Candy having found "drive".

She speeds us away, hysterical behind the wheel. Taking a sharp right, we drift around a corner block.

I look back, knowing this ain't good, and sit back, placing my hand on one of Candy's on the steering wheel. 'Candy— woah, take it easy. Everything's okay.'

She nods apprehensively.

* * *

I'm behind the wheel now. Candy stares a million miles away, lost, trembling in the passenger seat. This wasn't the plan, but I had no choice except to take her with me. We head down the A3, towards the south coast, towards Eleanor.

Candy sits up in an agitated state. 'Where're you going?' she asks, concerned, her breathing panicked.

I hesitate to say, but she's already guessed before I can utter a word.

'No—stop this!'

I shrug. 'I'm on the freeway.'

'No—no—get off!' she shouts, panicking and grasping at the door handle.

'Everythin's fine—you're in shock—'

'I'm not. I want out. Now! Please!'

'Alright—Alright. I'll get off at the next exit. Just stop—sit back!' I shout as I pull off.

It's been ten minutes, but something's changed in her. She can compartmentalise her regular line of work, but death and violence… maybe a person can only truly turn a blind eye to one thing and not many. She seems to have calmed down. I take a right and pull up in front of some local servo mechanic. She looks over at me.

'I need to go.'

'What're you talkin' about…where?—the Drum? Police are dead, Candice! There are witnesses.

We fucked up.' *I fucked up.* My eyes drift from her. 'I fucked up.'

'I'm sorry, I can't express myself at the moment…but I'm not going with you.' I look back at her. Something has changed—*Why does this feel like a breakup?*

'Candice. Police could be waiting.'

'I'm not going to stay there, but I need my stuff. I'll be quick—but I'm not asking you to stay either. I…think that we're on different paths.'

'Candice… I really don't—'

'My priorities have shifted.'

'So I'm supposed to just drop you off, and then what?'

'Then...you will go down your path, and I will go down mine.'

I look away. *This is crazy talk.* But I look back at her and nod. I turn the ignition and drive.

The last twenty-odd minutes between us have been quiet. Not a word said. I pull up about a block down the road from the Drum. I don't see police units, but they could still be in unmarked vehicles waiting inside. I sigh, thinking how stupid this is. *We shouldn't even be this close.*

Something she said earlier has stuck with me that I can't shake and I turn to her. 'What'd you mean earlier about priorities havin' changed and different paths?'

She doesn't look at me, taking her time to respond. 'Is what O'Leary said true...about you being a drug mule?' she asks, looking up at me.

Silence settles.

'Yeah,' she says with some satisfaction '...I remember Angel telling me you didn't like to talk much about your past.'

'She always told me it didn't matter to her either way.'

She nods slowly, looking away.

'But it does to you?'

She nods again, murmuring, 'I'm sorry.'

'You're a hooker-for fuck's sake, why should anythin' matter? It's not as if you've got a leg to stand on,' I bark back with spiteful defence, and I immediately know I've fucked up. I shouldn't have said that. *Where the hell did that come from?*

But it's too late. She's already out the door.

Fuck. I get out, calling for her, 'Candy!'

Eventually I catch up to her, 'Hey, listen—I'm sorry, okay!' But she shrugs me away.

I pull at her arm. She turns back, her eyes wild and gives me both barrels, 'I may fuck paying strangers to make a living, but that doesn't mean I'm okay with all that's bad in the world—and contrary to popular belief, not all sex workers are druggies…and you know this! I will not drag my son into it,' she cries, 'so I keep sober. I have to…it's where hope is, and if I lose that, I lose Oscar.'

That sound again—the rustle of tinsel and the chime of bells in the breeze—I look around and don't see either. Nothing stands out but the shop number of the bakery across the street, 888. *Hey Angel.*

Another sign: so I open up for the first time in a long time, 'I was Warehouse Coordinator in the Army Ordnance Corps, which is a fancy way of sayin' I was a box filler or shelf stacker. It's a non-technical entry-level gig for dead-shits like me. But…trouble's always had a way of findin' me.'

She looks at me curiously, wiping away tears. 'Is that how you learned to shoot a gun?'

'Yeah, they taught me all the same basic weapons trainin' as every other inductee into a unit—which was the best part.'

She nods and listens as I wax lyrical about a time I never got to share with Angel, a time I never really wanted to share with anyone, a time I wanted to bury so deep not even a zombie apocalypse would see it rise up.

Sighing, I continue, 'A couple of superiors approached me to run drugs, the kind you can't get a prescription for. So, for a little extra cash 'ere and there, I kept my mouth shut and eyes conveniently lookin' the other way as packages were loaded on and off army vehicles. Then, for some fuckin' reason, the higher-ups decided to send me to the other side of the world and station me in Afghanistan to continue my runs and shit-kickin' duties.

'I heard Afghanistan was the heroin capital of the world.' She offers.

I nod. 'But durin' that stint in the sand, I was a little sloppy with my box-fillin' and one of those packages had busted all over the back of a truck. This wouldn't have been too much of an issue, but this naive cadet asshole on one of his anal-retentive routine inspections looking to fast-track his way up the ranks saw the whole fuckin' calamity unfold. Long story short, the press got a hold of the incident and it became a national story that caused a shitstorm. The incident became a national story, and the press plastered me everywhere, makin' me the face of corrupt army drug smugglin' or some bullshit. I was dishonourably discharged...and lookin' at facin' jail time in the stockade,' I stop, feeling stupid. *I've said too much.*

We sit on the curb. Candy looks at me with sorrow; this's what I expected, which is why I've never opened up about it to anyone. I don't need people's sympathy.

She hugs me tight. 'I'm sorry Frank.'

I hug her back. 'Yeah...me too.'

Oddly, the mood feels lighter. Maybe talking does help? I'm not sure why I snapped at her like some judgmental prick. *I guess there's still a part of my old man in me.*

I doubt any of what I said's changed her mind, so I ask, 'How do I best contact you?'

She looks up, confused.

'My part of our deal...the money?'

'Oh, that...well, honestly,' she says, handing me a Siemens S45 mobile. 'Take this, and I'll text you. You're already taking my car, so what's a phone?' She shrugs. 'Not that it's mine in the first place. The amount of guys who leave their shit behind is crazy. Many of them don't even come back for it. And the ones that do, asking if we have a lost and found...'

She laughs. Silence settles again.

'Thanks for... Goodbye Frank.'

And just like that, she darts out of my life.

As I walk back to the car with my hands behind my back and the moon shining bright, I can't help but relive the night I was in custody waiting to be flown back home, the part of my story I keep to myself...the can of worms. Afghani rebels attacked the base. Since I was already cuffed, I became an easy target for them and they captured me. Little did they know I wasn't exactly priceless leverage to be bargained.

They held me captive for almost two years. I was starved, spat on, urinated on, shit on, beaten and tortured. With the barrel of an AK47 held at my head, I was forced to suck another man's cock more times than I'd like to remember while being sworn at in Arabic.

I spent countless nights weeping in the darkest corner of some cave under the desert. I remember trying to call back to my Catholic roots, mumbling the lord's prayer and begging for death to come. But God and I hadn't seen eye to eye in some time.

I knew the Australian Army would have much preferred me to stay missing and presumed dead. But by some chance, they came, and during their raid, I was found. My body was riddled with lesions. I could barely move and I couldn't speak due to blistering sores across my face and mouth. I was told I was unrecognisable. When I returned home, my discharge from the army remained, but all the charges and jail time were dropped. The two years of living in hell under the desert were considered enough punishment. The media humiliated me and the rebels broke me.

And then, I was tossed back into society without a cent to my name. The last seven years have been somewhat of an attempt to heal those deep wounds. Time went by quickly but progress was painfully slow. Then I met Angel, and that's when things changed. Time slowed, and progress sped up.

I HEAR IT COME

I think about how Eleanor must be living like a princess as I stare, hypnotised by the dark void of the Princes Highway. The car swallows the white highway lines underneath her. Although it remains a stinking hot night, rain falls, and the windshield steams.

Angel believed in fate—soulmates too. She made me a believer. At least I thought so till recently. I thought soulmates lived long lives together and if they didn't, they died together in each other's arms. Romeo and Juliet, that kinda thing.

I glance in the rearview mirror and notice droplets of someone else's blood on my neck and collar. I feel the tension in my grip on the steering wheel. My hands hurt. My knuckles are white, but I can't seem to loosen up. I don't want to loosen up.

Stripped by Depeche Mode plays on the radio. The highway road lines are hypnotic and I slip into a dream state: *the white highway lines split into two, then four, and then split again. The colour of the lines deepens to steel, like prison bars across the windshield. The windshield becomes murky, dimming out to darkness and leaving only the prison bars illuminated in the dark without shadow. The darkness beyond the bars fades, and the prison bars become bars to a steel gate. Moonlight shines beyond the gates, as they open to a steep paved driveway with lush green lawns on either side. Floating forward, like a phantom stranger, I see a clean, white, post-modernist mansion at the peak of the driveway. Large square windows are warmly lit from the inside, showcasing luxurious living. Marble steps lead to tall, thick, white doors that open to an entrance hall. In its centre, a staircase winds, and I move through it and see her. I see Eleanor. A princess, in a white swimsuit and silk robe. She turns away from me and proceeds up the staircase, each step in her white heels as confident as her next. Floating. Following. We're together now in a penthouse with a king-sized bed and a set of glass doors to a balcony, and she strides through. The view overlooks a coastline: cool blue water met by a white sand beach. Eleanor looks back over her shoulder. She's glamorous. I reach for her and my hands squeeze her throat. She becomes aroused. I feel my heart thumping. The fine line between pleasure and pain blurs as my grip tightens and mascara bleeds down her cheeks.*

She smirks, whispering, "It was the humane thing to do."

Louder, my heart thumps for the darkness to flow. My hands jerk tighter again and my thumbs dig hard into her jugular. I throttle her. Her face turns blue and her eyes bulge, bloodshot red. Wildly, she gasps for air, unable to release herself from my hands: chained to her neck and tightening more than a python's grip around its prey. I feel my face wince and my vision blurs with tears. I wheeze through pained gritted teeth, screaming, why? WHY?'—

The midi ringtone from a mobile phone alarms—a car horn blares from a passing vehicle—and I'm startled back to reality, quickly straightening back into the lane.

"It was the humane thing to do"—I remember what that monster said. My chest hurts, wounded with a deep black hole. My forehead and eyes ache from the intensity of revenge conjured in my mind's eye. Candy's mobile phone rings beside me in the passenger seat. I answer.

Her voice shakes with fear, in a state of panic. 'Frank! Frank!'

'What's wrong?'

'Please, you gotta turn around! O'Leary's back and he brought so many cops with him! They're all beating on us…' I hear a door being kicked open, followed by a struggle. The crackling of a phone drop and the sudden distant scream of Candy being dragged away. A moment of silence, then crackling, followed by heavy breaths on the other end of the line.

'Candy?' I stupidly ask.

A gruff 'Pfft,' is all I hear before disconnection and then silence.

I toss the phone aside and pull hard on the handbrake. The car screeches as I make a frantic ninety-degree turn, coming to a stop. Punching the accelerator pedal, grey smoke bellows from the back tyres as I enter the opposite lane and tear away back down the highway.

* * *

I pull off the Princes Highway back into Hurstville and the Polaroid image of Candy's son Oscar that she has taped to her dresser flashes before me. My mind becomes ultra-focused, visualising my approach to enter the Drum and rescue Candy.

I turn left into the petrol station behind the Drum, park, and take out Tweety to feed her. Then I hide her again in the old bloke's coat. I notice the station's red neon sign works again without a glitch, bleeding into the night sky—the stagnant smell of lamb on a spit in the air. I casually enter the petrol station and wince as my eyes adjust to its bright fluorescents.

Looking for the counter, I motion to the clerk, 'Bathroom?'

He points past me, answering in a thick Pakistani accent, 'To your left, but you'll need a key.'

He unhooks a bathroom key from a bolt screwed to a shelf behind him: a 7mm gear wrench attached like a keychain.

Handing it over, we nod at each other and I move quickly towards the bathroom in the back.

Inside, I lock the door behind me and move to the toilet stall. I shut the toilet lid, step up onto it and slide the window above open. Kicking out the wire mesh screen, I feed myself through the window, grasping onto the exterior pipes along the outside wall to help pull myself out. Using the same pipes, I climb to the roof.

The Drum's somewhat concealed and secure because of the high sheeted Colorbond fence topped with razor-wire in front of a row of pine trees that run along the property line within. I estimate there to be about a three to four meter concrete gap between the fence and the roof.

I think I can make the jump—*I have to!* Taking several steps back, I run towards the fence and leap, jumping over the gap…but fail to clear the fence cleanly and stack into a pine tree. Half my body thumps against the fence, tangling through the razor-wire and over into the pine branches. I hit the ground hard, pummelling my body, and the impact knocks the wind out of me.

I groan, hurt in the dark, laid out amongst fallen pine cones and all I want to do is stay here on the ground. But I think that for every breath I try to get back, Candy could be losing hers. So I sit my ass up and carefully remove a string of painful razor-wire from around my bleeding leg and pull the jagged pine cone out from under my ass.

I stagger across to a back window alongside a side door used for staff and peer between the aluminium black diamond grille. I see two heavily armed cops standing at the end of the hallway, both built like brick shit-houses, standing over Rongo and Aata who're cuffed back to back—they look defeated, beaten up and pissed off. I see several of the working girls tied up on the floor, with their faces turned away from me.

The girls suddenly curse, shout and cry out, 'Stop!' as

Madame Lacey is dragged out by her grey hair and tossed towards them by another brute cop.

She looks in shock and I can hear her distraught, in conversation with someone out of sight. '...I don't understand —you promised us!—'

Then I see O'Leary step forward from behind the two armed cops.

He crouches alongside her. 'Unlike what you do here, I don't facilitate false promises.'

He stands and motions for the surrounding pigs to lift her to her feet. Madame Lacey spits on O'Leary's face as she's dragged to her feet.

Without hesitation, he strikes her with a sucker punch to the gut while the other girls yell and shout, crying, 'Mum,' as Lacey drops to her knees, winded and sobbing.

I've seen enough! I reach into my pocket to draw Tweety, but she's not there—*Shit!*—she must've fallen out when I fell. I look back and see a trail of blood coming from my left leg leaving a path behind me. Following the blood trail back it leads me directly to Tweety. I pick her up and hear footsteps approach, bracing against the trunk of a pine tree in the pitch-black of night. I wait, watching a guy with the body of Arnold, strapped with a tactical vest and packing a pump-action shotgun, patrol.

He sees the blood trail and halts—*I don't have time for this shit.* Before I allow him to look over, see me and draw, I rush him and pop Tweety off, point-blank in his face—creating a third eye right where his nose used to be. Not wise, I've probably given myself away, so I move quickly, picking up the shotgun alongside the newly anointed corpse and dash to the back door.

Pocketing Tweety, I check the shotgun, *one in the chamber and four in the tube.* Looking up to the sky, I take a deep breath and notice a few of the brighter stars, wondering at what point they look away, if they even can—*now would be a good time.*

I shoot out the two hinges of the back door and kick it in, startling the already alarmed cops inside. Shouldering the shotgun, I rush through the back hallways, past the kitchen, firing two rounds for effect. O'Leary cowers away out of sight. One cop takes cover while another charges forward, aiming his pistol, but before he can get a shot off, I blow half his head away with the last round. He drops like the sack of shit he is—blood and pieces of brain smearing against a wall, reminiscent of a Jackson Pollock piece.

I drop the spent shotgun and take cover, drawing my Tweety Bird, and count the bullets that the panicked cop wastes, trying to take me out quickly. I think I have it, *maybe 17 rounds… and from a Glock 17 with a standard clip… that means he's empty…*

I poke my head out and am unexpectedly struck. A bullet pierces my left ear and blasts a hole in the wall behind me, leaving splinters in the back of my head. I grit my teeth and flinch, retaking cover. Tinnitus hums loudly. *Fuck-goddammit! Never was good at math. Like I wasn't already pissed off, now I feel stupid too.*

Fuck this cunt! I jump out from behind the wall and assail the rotten pig. Tweety does her thing, leaving the fucker in a pool of blood. I look up and see O'Leary scamper up the staircase.

Picking Madame Lacey up, I assist her quickly out of harm's way as bullets whiz past from obscured cops, hiding throughout the Drum. I yell at the girls to stay the fuck down, but one of them doesn't listen and, in her erratic attempt to escape, the bullets turn her into Swiss cheese, causing her to slump to the ground only a few feet from where she started. The girls who keep down cry, screaming the dead girl's name.

'STAY THE FUCK DOWN!' I shout again.

Lacey and I duck behind the bar, and I glance at her. 'Stay 'ere—you have good cover.'

She nods, her eyes wild with panic.

Looking around, I see Nicky's crumpled, dead body: a .32

Colt alongside him — *Goddamnit, Nicky, why'd you hafta go be a hero?* He must've reached for the Colt when the cops gate-crashed.

Bullets hail overhead as shards of mirror and shattered glass bottles rain over Madame Lacey and me from the back bar wall. We look at each other—me sorrowful—her petrified and trembling.

'I'm sorry!' I shout over the din.

But she won't have it, shaking her fear off for just a moment and shouting back, 'Get these cunts!'

Between the gunfire, I hear the girls up on the second floor scream and shout and my patience wanes. I see a toolbox underneath the bar sink and yank it out.

Inside is a heavy-duty pipe wrench. *Perfect!* Leaping to my feet, I fire several rounds, not expecting to take out any of the boys in blue but to allow myself to see where they're hiding, thanks to Tweety's muzzle flash lighting up the joint.

I see several and jump the bar to deal with each of the *Cuntstables* with the wild, uncontrolled savagery of an ancient Norse warrior in close quarters, whipping my pipe wrench into skulls and across frail chins, along with point-blank gunshot blasts to the chests and abdomens, pushing upstairs towards Candy's room.

Spent bullet casings fall alongside shattered teeth. A loose tooth hits me in the eye with a splatter of dirty pig blood across my face, and I'm suddenly blinded, shouting obscenities. Suddenly, I'm shoved and my arms are locked up, clenched in a struggle, shoved against the wall on the second floor, and both Tweety and the bloody, flesh-matted wrench fall from my grip.

I can't see shit, but I can tell this pig has at least 15 to 20 kilos on me, and I think he's broken one of my ribs. With my left hand, I'm able to pull his forearm away from against my neck and quickly capitalise with a clean head-butt, stunning him. I head-butt him again and again — *ah, fuck it one more time for good measure.* Blood somehow clears from my eyes and I see him fall backward over the railing. His neck snaps as he hits the floor below, looking like something from Picasso's Cubism period.

I've lost the wrench, but pick up Tweety. I stalk towards Candy's room, heaving like a bloodthirsty zombie in a brothel bathed in blood. I am drenched with the grime of rotten pigs, black and blue, and maybe have a broken rib or two—and my left leg is torn to shit from the razor-wire fence. Much of my hate and rage has been spent, but not all. I have plenty of reserves.

I swing open the door, Tweety aimed, ready to chirp, and in the middle of the room I see Candy on her knees facing me, in tears, with a black eye, her swollen lips forcibly swathed around the end of a pistol, held near O'Leary's crotch as he stands alongside her, smirking.

'Don't turn on the light, Sonny. You wouldn't wanna see mummy and daddy playing bang-bang.'

I glare at him, seething and unamused. He dares me to do something about it, but I don't—not yet.

He nods at Tweety. 'Drop it, Frank.'

I try, but I can't quite seem to let go of Tweety physically.

Frozen, I mutter gruffly, 'Can't do that,' knowing he won't understand.

He forces the barrel deeper down Candy's throat. But I just can't let go of Tweety. It's as if she's fused to me. The two of us glare at each other in a stalemate with only the sound of Candy's whimpers. The wail of police sirens emerges, and the sight of their flare outside the window soon follows. I don't know what to do but hold aim. Candy looks at me with pleading eyes and I stand there as O'Leary continues, edging to pull the trigger.

'You're delusional,' he barks.

'What's that?' I ask.

'You're delusional. That Angel was just another hooker. It was her job to make you think she loved you. She sure as hell loved me too. It's what they do—that's what they all do.'

I glare wrathfully—hate is all I know. It's all the wolf feeds on, and it's all I have to give him—to give the world.

The sirens grow louder—they're just outside. I hear the front door crash, splintered apart, and a horde of boot steps storm up the stairs. I'm suddenly jumped by several cops and brought down. The cops press my face into the floor and dig their knees into my neck and back. Someone forcibly rips Tweety from my hands, and it hurts. Out of the corner of my eye, I see O'Leary release the pistol fellatio from Candy, and, like some toy he no longer wants to play with, he pushes her aside.

It becomes harder to breathe as I'm cuffed, the sound of everything dulls, and my vision begins to blur and fade… I'm drowning…dreaming: *passionate kisses, lazy sex—a bright Sunday morning in bed holdin' Angel close. We laugh and she lights my world up by smilin' at me.* There's a muffled racket—an uproar—Candy's shouting. Suddenly, as if pulled out of the depths of the sea, I can breathe, see and hear again. I look up from the floor and am taken aback. Candy wields a pistol aimed at O'Leary's head. He's humiliated again: his hands on top of his head.

'Un-cuff him—un-cuff him!' Candy shouts.

Officers scramble to un-cuff me.

'Now back off him—back away! Get-up-Frank—GET UP!'

I drag myself off the floor and glance behind me.

Several armed cops, with their weapons raised, are itching to put Candy down, but they try to reason with her.

'You don't know what you're doing!' shouts one.

'Put that gun on the ground.' Demands another.

'C'mon Frank!' she shouts again.

I step over to the opposite side of the room alongside her.

'You fuck,' snaps O'Leary, 'what're you gonna do? There's nowhere you can hide. You're both fucked!'

I stare at O'Leary, knowing he's right, but Candy has a son who needs her.

'Frank, what do we do?' she asks me, the pistol trembling

in her hands as police opposite us shout for her to put it down.

She looks at me again, with those pleading Sanpaku eyes of hers. I look behind us, to the window—it's the only way out.

'Tweety, where is she?' I say to the row of cops across from me, but they look confused.

'My gun! Where is it? Give it to me.'

One cop slowly removes Tweety from behind his jacket and tosses it to me. I take O'Leary away from Candy, twisting one of his hands to breaking point, and shove Tweety's beak into his back as he squirms. I motion to her that we're leaving through the window.

'Out the window?' She asks, wide-eyed.

I nod, focusing on the row of pigs. She steps through the windowsill onto the fire escape. I follow, stepping backwards, O'Leary still my human shield.

'I'm not fucking going anywhere, cunt!' he states.

I twist out his left hand and pull, Tweety chirps, blasting his index and middle fingers off. He howls, shocked, and cries for his fellow piggies not to shoot. They all do as they're told.

'...Okay!—Okay!' O'Leary sobs.

Complying, I pull O'Leary through the window with me. Candy races down ahead of us as I push and shove O'Leary forward. We reach the ground and I look around to see if it's clear—O'Leary takes his chance, breaking free and pulling out a .38 snubnose from a concealed leg strap. But I catch wind of it in time and we grasp each other's wrists with our free hands, wrestling like some strength test, trying to aim our pistols at each other's heads. O'Leary fires a shot and my ears ring. Pissed off, I break the bro-fight code and throw my knee hard into his nuts, spin quickly and throw an elbow uppercut at his jaw, catching the .38 in my hand as he drops to the concrete below—knocked out cold.

The officers above shout for us to halt as they race down the fire escape... I grab Candy by the hand and together we run down the laneway while other officers from the window open fire. We dash around the fence and into the petrol station towards her parked car.

There, we scramble into it, slamming the doors behind us. I throw O'Leary's .38 at Candy's feet in an agitated state and floor the car in reverse, dodging oncoming vehicles. I rip the gear into drive and thrash the car in escape, headed towards the highway.

I slow my breathing with controlled breaths and look over to Candy, staring blankly in shock toward nothing—I think she no longer has room to compartmentalise.

* * *

I stop myself asking her if she's alright because I know she's not and she knows I care anyway. Right now, the best thing is to have the most straightforward sounds, like the thrum of this car driving down the highway, to ease her and it will come.

* * *

Hypnotised again by the dark void of the Princes Highway, I hear it come—Candice cries. I give her a moment, then affectionately place my hand on her. She drops her hands from her face, looks over and leans across the seat into me. I put my arm around her and for the rest of the drive, we hold each other.

* * *

It was Angel's figure that had me smitten as she walked towards me on that crisp evening wearing a short black skirt and a taut black leather jacket, a curious smile on her face... those gorgeous round eyes of hers—so damn sexy. I remember saying to myself, god damn this is my type of girl.

100

She asked if I smoked, wanting to bum a cigarette from me. As I came to find out, she never bought a pack of cigarettes in her entire life—there was always some dummy willing to give her one. Can't blame the poor suckers. I only had one cigarette left that night, so we shared a smoke—lighting it with her white disposable BIC, the 27 Club kind. Now in my possession within the old bloke's coat pocket, close to my chest. We talked for hours and laughed too. I'd experienced nothing like it. Two strangers on a rooftop bar. *What did she ever see in me?*

We've been on the road for over an hour. Candy dozed off a while back. We're in the Gong now. Eleanor's last known address is somewhere along a beach or a lake off Windang. I'll leave Candy in the car; hopefully, she doesn't wake up. Hopefully, I go in, find Eleanor, and… Hopefully, Candy wakes up to the large amounts of money I promised for her and Oscar, so they can start a new life somewhere else, away from everything shit.

I make a stop near the Warilla Hotel. *I think I'm lost*—I've gone too far and missed it. I turn back up Shellharbour Rd and onto Windang Rd. The location is on my left, just a few short minutes away. I feel my heart thumping as I slow the car and approach my destination. But I'm confused and feel lost as I pull into a small independent petrol station that appears out of time. It's closed and dimly lit. I park and get out of the car, careful not to wake Candy, and look around. But I don't see too much. It's pitch black. I turn the headlights on and they reveal an entrance to an inn behind the station.

I walk over to the sign near the road, I notice that the address doesn't match what I've been given. I can't help but think I've been duped—*Did O'Leary send me on a wild goose chase?*

I head back to the car, turn off the headlights, and think through the situation while watching Candy sleep in the passenger seat. It's quiet, with no one and no traffic in sight. The digital clock on the dashboard displays 4:44 am. *Hey*

Angel. I gather the old bloke's coat and lay it over Candy, tucking it around her, grab Tweety, get out of the car and gently close the driver-side door behind me.

I stare blankly listening to the rustling of gum tree branches from down the road. My memories of Angel are now like monochromatic water paintings—fading. This feels like an ending.

GUM TREE

Kurt and Ellie scamper through the underbrush, whipping past rustling branches, scratching and clawing at their skin and clothes as they push through the bushland as if escaping an impending tide. The crimson glow from the taillights intensifies, cutting through the darkness like malevolent eyes. The dry leaves and twigs beneath their feet crackle and pop like distant fireworks. Ellie slows down to a stop, bent over to catch her breath. The smell of eucalyptus fades as she detects the scent of unleaded in the air. Gazing up, she sweeps a lush branch obstructing her view from out of her way, and her posture stiffens. Kurt catches up—standing equally shocked alongside her, confronted by the horror before them.

Precariously wrapped around a rooted gum tree perched on the edge of a hazardous cliff, a mangled car wreck teeters in the dark. It threatens to tumble down into a rock-strewn, rapid river just below the precipice at any moment. Chunks of hard plastics, shattered glass and sharp debris are scattered throughout. Steam hisses and liquid froths from the wreck's cracked radiator, spilling across its hot engine. The industrial smell of car parts cooked in coolant lingers in the air. The red taillights are bright, casting an eerie glow, filling the atmosphere like a hazard warning not to approach a scene of imminent danger, all accompanied by the restless sounds of creaking wood and steel, like that of a forsaken sea vessel at night.

They walk stiffly as if their minds have detached from their bodies, frozen in time from just minutes ago, observing their physical selves inching closer to confront the harrowing wreck. Kurt reaches the passenger's side and warily peers inside. His heartbeat races as he recoils. Ellie's unable to resist her morbid curiosity and peeks inside after him, but she quickly looks away too, catching her breath as she averts her eyes. The gruesome scene is too much to bear.

Inside the wreck, the driver, Frank, is a gruesome mess. His body is blood-soaked and limp. His face is mostly buried against the steering wheel, with only a mangled fraction exposed. In the passenger seat is a woman, Angel, pallid, her body wilted, with blood oozing from her hairline. The shattered glass within, scattered haphazardly like popcorn, resembles the debris in a cinema after a screening. Frank and Angel appear to be dead.

The dryness in Kurt's mouth hinders him from swallowing—sweat beads on his clammy forehead. His hand trembles as he reaches into his pocket, but fumbles.

'I'm gonna call for help,' he stammers through a dry, raspy throat. He drops his phone but quickly retrieves it. Turning away from Ellie, he dials with shaky fingers.

'Yes...an ambulance...a car accident...I think they're dead!'

Ellie peers back over her shoulder at the perched wreck. She collects herself with a shake of her hands and a concentrated breath.

With a hushed tone, she says, 'I'll check their pulse,' and minding the shattered glass, she cautiously steps towards the car. Peering inside, her heart is heavy with dread. She focuses first on Frank. Overwhelmed. She's unsure of where to begin but reaches in. Using her index and middle fingers, she presses them against Frank's bloody, wet neck and holds her breath, seeking any sign of life, but there's nothing, no pulse. Thinking she has it wrong, she slides her misplaced, blood-caked fingers further under his neck and holds, maintaining pressure. Her dejected expression deepens; still no signs of life. She pulls away, looking at Angel but lingers momentarily, captured by Angel's resemblance to herself. Determined, she carefully manoeuvres around the shattered glass as she makes her way around the wreck.

At the passenger side, Ellie pauses, unnerved by how genuinely similar they appear: the colour of their hair, the angle of their jawline and even the contour of their lips. *"This could've been me,"* she thinks.

Reaching in to check Angel's pulse, she pauses, her attention caught by something in Angel's hand, fluttering between her bloody fingers is a crumpled piece of paper. Recognition of what it appears to be dawns in Ellie's eyes. She looks up beyond the maimed couple through the driver's side to Kurt, who's pacing in circles on the phone with emergency services.

'Like I said, two people inside. A man and a woman. That's right, about 20 Ks from the Industry Petrol Station...' he continues, relaying their location.

Ellie's attention returns to the crumpled piece of paper. She momentarily hesitates but decides to investigate, reaching for the paper. The wreck groans ominously; the gum tree creaks and branches snap. She freezes, contemplating whether to retreat. But after a brief pause, the sounds subside, and she attempts once more to pluck the paper from Angel's grip. Cautiously, she leans in and stretches out her hand, pinching the corner as jagged glass catches her top, tearing a hole. She ignores it. Determined, she extracts the piece of paper from Angel's bloodied hand.

Stepping away from the wreck with a mix of intrigue and anxiety, Ellie carefully unfurls the crumpled paper. In a matter of seconds, her eyes widen with disbelief. She darts to the back of the vehicle and crouches against one of the red tail-lights. Her hands jitter, feeling her heart pound loud enough that she can hear it. She scans the numbers on her hand against the crumpled paper and her mouth falls open with giddy astonishment. In her possession is a blood-stained, winning lottery ticket.

Kurt looks past the wreck and reports, 'Ambulance is on the way! ...Ellie?' He can't see her, and concern creeps into his voice as he shouts, 'ELLIE?'

Slowly, she rises from behind the wreck, her eyes fixed on the ticket in her hand.

'Ellie?' he approaches with worry etched on his face, 'You okay? What is it?'

Softly, she whimpers, 'It's a winner.'

Straining to hear, he leans closer, 'What? Speak up.'

She looks at him bewildered and proclaims, 'This lottery ticket...it's a winner.'

'What're you talking about? I thought you lost?'

'No! The woman had it in her hand,' she says, passing the ticket to him. 'Look!' He looks at the ticket, confused; trying to process the revelation.

'It's a winner, Kurt.'

'What? Are you sure—I mean, how do you know?'

She nods vigorously. 'The numbers, they match,' showing her hand with the winning numbers inscribed in black ink.

Kurt takes her hand and aligns the ticket alongside it, scrutinising the numbers across both. Suddenly, it hits him— stepping back in amazement; he combs his fingers through his hair and gazes at her in sheer disbelief.

He gasps, shocked. 'Holy shit.'

Smiles spread across their faces. Overwhelmed by a sensational thrill, they spontaneously burst into shocked laughter —they can't believe their luck. But their elation soon dwindles, as they stand in the sticky unease, shattered glass crunching beneath their shoes, the presence of the car wreck in front of them: the grim reality of lifeless bodies inside. They're forced to snap back to reality. In the tranquil sounds of branches gently swaying with various nocturnal creature sounds of the night, they solemnly gaze upon the wreck as the weight of the situation settles on them.

'They must've been speeding,' Ellie says, tinged with insincerity.

Kurt looks at his wife with suspended breath. Her gaze is unyielding and cold as she stares at the wreckage. Conflicted, he looks sorrowfully at the winning lottery ticket, wrestling with his conscience.

'Yeah…maybe,' he finally replies, 'We can't keep it.'

'They're dead.'

'Yeah, I know, but…what if—maybe they have kids?'

'Do you see a booster seat in the back? I don't.'

His expression becomes pensive, and he avoids eye contact with her. 'They could be older?'

'There's luggage in the backseat…they were probably on a road trip or a holiday.'

'Or running away.' he adds.

'You know who buys lottery tickets—you know who does? Losers. Losers buy lottery tickets—losers like us. I bought one.' She snatches the ticket from him. 'You gotta be in it to win it, right? Well, we're in it—and we're not losers anymore.'

'Jesus, Ellie,' he murmurs.

'We won the lottery.'

'Did we?'

'We won…' At that moment, Angel's voice breaks through from inside the wreck, a sobbing plea for help.

Kurt and Ellie freeze, startled and unsure if they heard anything. They lean in, straining their ears, listening more closely to the sounds inside the wreck. An ominous atmosphere breezes through, rustling the leaves. They hear it again: Angel cries for help. Panicked, Kurt looks at Ellie; there is no mistaking the call for help this time. The clammy sickness he felt earlier in the night returns, breaking him into a cold sweat, but he nears the wreck anyway and peers inside. Ellie joins him, her expression distant. Angel coughs up blood, and then ever so slightly, with glassy eyes, a tear runs down her pale cheek. She looks at them.

'I can't...feel anything,' she confesses with a breathless sob.

Ellie steps away, distancing herself in shock, with a wary look.

Kurt moves forward. 'It's okay. I called for help. An ambulance is on the way.' Glancing to his left, he expects his wife to be there, but she isn't; she's further behind, seemingly conversing with herself.

'Ellie?' he approaches, gently taking hold of her arm, 'Hey—'

'We can still keep it!' she desperately interrupts.

'What? What're you talking about? We can't keep the ticket. She's alive!'

'Alive? You heard what that woman said. She can't feel anything!'

'Which is why we can't keep it, Ellie. She'll need the money to help her.'

'Help her what, move again?'

'Yes! What the hell's wrong with you? You're not thinking straight!'

'No! You're not thinking straight! That's not a life.'

'What're you saying?'

'How's she gonna live? Bound to a wheelchair for the rest of life, paralysed from the neck down in some lonely mansion? That's not a life, that's not living! But we...' She steps back, stalling, shutting her eyes tight with a pained expression before taking a deep breath.

He watches her, puzzled by her apparent conflicting emotions.

She opens her eyes and tenderly reaches out. '...but we can live, baby,' caressing his cheek.

Confused and still grappling with shock, he stares at her, unable to speak. Ellie leans in closer again, her touch coaxing him as he anxiously avoids eye contact. She gently lifts his chin to meet her gaze as it transforms into something more sultry and seductive, captivating him.

'Just you and me, baby. Travelling all over the world… playing your music.'

Her eyes exude a new and alluring confidence, a feeling she's never experienced before that makes her feel sexy, dangerous, and irresistible. Kurt's attention shifts from her captivating gaze to her moist, pouty lips, and he becomes entranced, unable to resist her allure.

'And fucking anywhere you want,' she says uninhibitedly, without blushing.

His body experiences a swell of desire and his heart stirs darkly in a way it hasn't before, as if something primal within him has ignited. Lost in Ellie's dark and alluring eyes, his loins swell, and at that moment, he's mesmerised.

Abruptly, the sobbing cough from Angel pulls him back to the grim reality of the situation. He turns toward Angel injured inside the wreck, but Ellie firmly clasps his face, bringing his attention back to her. She kisses him intensely. The kiss is unlike anything a typical married woman would ever do; it's more like the seduction of a wicked vampire. A "spell" washes over him. She lightly bites his lower lip as she steadily pulls away, their eyes locked in a passionate and intense gaze.

Another breeze whispers through the trees, this time carrying the faint sound of emergency sirens. She tunes in on the distant sirens and abruptly breaks away from him, her eyes wide, darting and panicked, forced to think on her feet, muttering under her breath. She takes his hand with a look of desperation.

'One fucking break, right, baby?' she reminds him, 'just you and me.'

He nods, staring vacantly, still under the fog of arousal, his mind clouded.

She tilts her head, her expression shifting as an idea possesses her and softly she says, 'Suffocation.'

Unease twitches in Kurt's eyes. He glances at the wreck, pressing his lips in uncertainty.

Suddenly, the haunting, sorrowing plea said to him the last time he saw his father returns, whispering in his mind, "Girls come and go, mate. Don't throw us away."

'It's the humane thing to do,' Ellie asserts.

His eyes glaze and become distant—the planted idea sprouting quickly, taking root. He nods. His blank expression indicates he's wholly convinced. He turns towards the wreck, his thoughts consumed by a cruel resolve. Angel is nervous and unable to move as she fearfully watches him enter her line of sight, framed by the crooked passenger-side door. His gaze is intense, his dark eyes wide and unrelenting as he silently looks down at her. Leaning closer, he braces Angel against the seat with one arm and reaches toward her face with the other. She pleads, her voice shrill, sobbing in distress. Her breath quickens, bursting in and out as if trying to swallow air, and her damp eyes fill with a desperate plea for help. He is relentless and unyielding, firmly pinching her nose and clasping Angel's mouth shut, sealing her plea in silence.

Ellie stands by, motionless with an eerie detachment, watching the scene unfold. Without warning, Angel's limp body spasms and her eyes grow dull as life slips away. The dark eyes of Frank stare blankly, a silent witness to the murder taking place.

Kurt's complexion is pallid and clammy, his arms tense as he maintains a tight grip across Angel's face. She lasts another several long seconds, her eyes eventually rolling back into her head. It's over. He continues to hold his grip, paralysed by the act he has committed, unable to release Angel's lifeless form.

'Kurt,' Ellie gently says, offering him a nod that seems to grant permission to let go. He complies and begins to tremble as he slowly releases his grip on the lifeless passenger; groaning with post-murder clarity—but suddenly, without warning, Frank, mangled and blood-soaked, heaves for breath, as if touched by some unearthly force. A sudden surge of energy courses through him, and Frank seizes Kurt's arm tightly. With uncanny strength, he drags Kurt deeper into the wreck, roaring like a vengeful zombie pulling a living man into his grave.

Kurt's legs dangle as he desperately kicks through the passenger-side window, unable to free himself, shrieking for Ellie. 'Help! Help me!'

Startled by the sudden turn of events, she springs forward to help but stops abruptly when the weight of the wreck causes the ground underneath it to shift with wrenching snaps and cracks. The gum tree's trunk uproots and topples into the river stream with a thunderous splash, its long roots remain attached to the dirt crater it leaves behind. The wreck follows, sliding down the trunk toward the river, but a front tyre gets caught, wedged between branches, preventing the wreck from plummeting. It hangs dangerously suspended: Kurt is trapped inside. The howling sound of emergency sirens draws nearer.

Ellie's head tilts once more, and the treacherous situation suddenly becomes an opportunity in her mind, unfolding another dark plot. Calculated and swift, she approaches the bank's perilous edge and notes the rushing water below. She measures the distance between herself and the wreck as she peers into the twisted vehicle. Inside, she sees Frank, menacing. His teeth grit and his eyes pulse with purpose and rage, holding Kurt captive, his grip unwavering. Kurt's trapped and terrified, and he screams incoherently, unable to break free; squirming inside.

He throws his head back, staring at her, his eyes wild and cries to his wife, 'Fucking help me!'

With a deep breath, she summons her strength and delivers a forceful front kick to the wreck. The lodged tyre shifts but doesn't dislodge fully. The strobing shards of red and blue lights from emergency services gleam nearer. Daunted by the fact that time is running out, she takes another deep breath and kicks the wreck as hard as possible. The front tyre dislodges. The force of the motion sends her tumbling backward to the ground. The wreck slides off the trunk and plummets into the river below, sinking quickly as a mighty rush of water engulfs it.

Ellie watches the scene with an adrenaline-fuelled glow in her eyes. The noise of the river drowns out any screams. She remains breathless and devoid of remorse as the river swallows the last remnants of the wreck, leaving behind an eerie silence and a sense of finality.

Torches slash lines into the night as paramedics emerge from the bushland behind, her stark stare transforming into a torrent of blubbered crocodile tears.

She turns, collapsing into the arms of a burly paramedic. 'He—he was trying to help,' she stammers amidst bogus tears, her sobs echoing through the night.

The bewildered paramedic embraces her tightly, offering, 'It's alright darl, you're okay—you're safe.'

Another equally bewildered, rake-thin paramedic quickly radios for rescue crews to hustle toward the cliff edge.

* * *

Emergency rescue vehicles and personnel with bright flak jackets mill at the scene—the recovery operation is already well in progress. Filling the air is the sound of a rescue helicopter hovering overhead—a spotlight shines from the chopper across the area, focusing its beam on the now calm river. A cable truck with a hoist fixed to its trailer cranks as it winds a thick cable leading off the cliff's edge and into the river. The cable line becomes taut, and emergency personnel stand by, ready. Bubbling swamp-like sounds emanate from the water, creating an eerie atmosphere. The car wreck begins to emerge, and the water drains away, revealing three lifeless bodies within. Kurt's corpse lies draped across the unmoving bodies of Angel and Frank, his face swollen and dull, blue in some spots, purple in others. Using the jaws of life, emergency personnel work to pry open the crumpled door of the twisted, watery wreck.

Ellie sits in the back of an ambulance, wrapped in a thermal blanket. An officer hands her a hot cup of coffee as a paramedic attends to her. Abrupt shouts from the wreck catch everyone's attention and emergency personnel rush towards it.

She freezes with uncertainty, asking, 'What's going on?'

Just as the officer is about to reply, crackling words interrupt from the radio fixed to his belt. "All personnel required." The paramedic quickly grabs a medical kit bag beside her and, with another officer, they rush away, leaving Ellie seated, clutching a steaming cup of coffee. She watches, nervous twitches swimming up and down her, unable to see past the crowd of reflective flak jackets and hard hats as they pass a basket stretcher toward the wreck.

Incredibly, Frank is somehow barely alive. Water and blood drain from his mouth as emergency personnel carefully lift him from the wreckage and onto a basket stretcher.

The thermal blanket slips off Ellie's shoulder as he's carried past her. She digs a hand into her pocket to retrieve the winning, blood-stained lottery ticket. Her posture has an unnatural stillness, and she feels the ticket's thin, crinkled texture between her thumb and index fingers as she stares vacantly into the void.

JUST LIKE YOU IMAGINED

It was like a sudden comedown. He was darkly agitated and in pain one minute but he was briskly snatched by a feeling so vast that it drowned out the distinct sounds of whispering gum trees in the hot breeze blowing from beyond the lake and the mountains.

The sensation dulls to pure noiselessness, actualising itself with a tingling throughout his face, accompanied by a warmth across his brow. His wide eyes well and the tingling gushes underneath his skin coursing through each limb. Paused, outside a shut petrol station, forty-something-year-old Frank Conway is in peaceful communion with what might be his last moments alive.

It's a little over an hour till sunrise, and, like a jogger before dawn, it's all quiet except for the crunch of gravel under Frank's feet as he paces down the entranceway of the South Pacific Park Village. He scopes out the reception and peers inside through the glass door, seeing a single desk lamp lighting the check-in desk. He studies the grounds for any sign of activity for the next minute. Convinced enough, he walks back and, fortunately, finds a gap in a window left open. Carefully and quietly, he lifts the window open and climbs through.

Inside, Frank gently proceeds to the desk behind a yellowing CRT monitor. He taps the keyboard and a login pane appears on the screen. Someone foolishly attached a Post-It note to the monitor with the login password "Village01". Frank navigates the hotel software, selects the "Guest" tab and types "Eleanor" but pauses.

'Shit, what's her last name?' he grumbles under his breath.

Frank clicks "Enter" anyway, hoping for some luck. The result lists several Eleanors, but none of them registered as currently occupied. The most recent was a year ago. He thinks for a moment, combing his fingers through his blood-matted hair and returns to the monitor, typing "Ellie", and taps "Enter". A single search result returns Neff and Ellie: Cabin 10. And she appears to be booked for the next three months.

Frank tiptoes the park grounds. The shallow ripple of water echoes from along the bank and the descending full moon illuminates the pale blue shabby appearance of Cabin 10—the last cabin in a row along the lake that sits isolated on a grassy field between two large trees.

He pauses, his gaze fixed on the cabin. Someone concealed and draped the windows from the inside. However, a blue light flickers between a slither of drawn blinds. Pulling his pistol, he approaches with muted caution, stepping onto the small wooden patio to the front door. He feels the slightest creak underneath his feet. He leans forward and listens for any signs inside. He can hear indistinct music: a recognisable song he can't quite put his finger on.

Gently, he twists the door handle. It unlocks. He creeps the door open with his pistol aimed and steps inside. The room is unkempt and dirty. No one has cleaned it in some time. There's a stagnant smell of body odour and mildew. A television set fixed to the wall across from an unmade bed quietly plays *Glory Box* by Portishead on ABC's music video show **rage.** Just beyond the bed is a door to a bathroom. It's open. The light is on. A woman groans from within.

His demeanour is cold and unblinking. Paying attention to each step, he cautiously and quietly makes his way towards the bathroom, but a red Gideon's bible catches his attention on the bedside table.

God ain't savin' you, I won't let him. He peers inside the bathroom with his finger on the trigger and one eye aimed through his pistol's sights. Ellie sits in a bathtub and to his dismay she is sickly pale and gaunt. Several unhealed puncture wounds are visible on her left arm, bound with a kettle cord. She holds a needle filled with crystal junk she was just about to shoot in her arm. This Ellie is a stark contrast to the attractive young woman seen in photos from the police report.

She pauses, looks up, and her gaze lingers on him blankly. Neither says a word as *Glory Box* continues.

'Put that down.' he instructs.

She looks away to the tiled wall across from her and as if speaking to someone, says, 'You did it again,' and drops the needle.

'Eleanor...Eleanor Neff?' he gruffs.

Her face softens as a tear runs down her pale cheek.

Knowing this day would come, relieved, she gently whispers, 'Frank...'

On Windang Road, a flare of light passes across Candy. It wakes her, and she basks in that brief moment of blissful unawareness, that moment that falls away so quickly, as memories from only several hours ago flash and align with her foreign surroundings. She sits up, her breath fraught with anxiety. The light is from a police vehicle that pulls up. She swiftly sinks, shrinking into her seat, panicked.

The police vehicle idly sits in the dark as if the car, with its own mind, is staring at her. She cautiously peers through the windscreen as the police vehicle slowly rolls forward down the road and enters South Pacific Park Village. Aware of Frank's coat over her, she realises he must be somewhere in the caravan park. Checking the coat pockets, she finds nothing. She looks around and pauses with a shallow gasp. Looking down at her feet, a nervous quiver in her bottom lip, she carefully picks up O'Leary's .38.

In cabin 10, Frank rattles off questions without pause, like a machine gun defending a battle line. But the only thing under attack is his preconceived notions of Ellie. Feeling defeated and annoyed by the music playing on the TV, he quickly turns and fires at it—the screen pops, fragmenting like a spider's web, with a smoking hole at its centre.

Outside, an alarmed flock of Galahs flies from a tree at the end of the park near cabin 10 and over the lake as dawn peeks its head over the mountains, tinging the sky red. The police vehicle quietly pulls to a halt.

In cabin 10, Frank shakes his head. 'I don't understand.'

'Does it matter?' asks Ellie.

His fingers tense around his pistol's grip. 'You killed her.'

She gently nods. 'I died that day too—'

He pounces on her and she flinches. Shoving his pistol into her head, he roars, 'NO!'

She cries, 'A love for someone you could run away with— a love for someone you could run away with,' cowering in the bathtub, her eyes tightly shut.

He steps back. Ellie continues repeatedly; her words seem to have some cut-through, making sense to him. She softly opens her eyes and faces him.

'He wasn't someone you could run away with. He was…,' she drifts off, looking back at the corner of the bathroom across from her, afraid to continue as if Kurt were there listing. But then she picks up her words somewhere else, 'Things just came to light after we got married…'

Frank listens but the ongoing dialogue within his head distracts him—voices perched upon each of his shoulders duelling.

'But I just made life worse when the car went into the ravine,' she says, before stopping herself from continuing.

His attention returns to her and she looks at him blankly. 'I didn't win the lottery…I stole it,' she says, 'and since then, he's been everywhere. I tried so many times, oh god, I tried to leave, but I couldn't get away. Somehow, he always stops me…even now. I know he brought you.'

She looks to that corner of the bathroom once again, but this time, she brings Frank into her vision: the chilling spectral of Kurt. Frank's stomach churns, bearing witness to a wet corpse with tattered clothes, his rotting skin purple and blue and his eyes lonely and unblinking—a zombie from the marsh.

'Every day I was with you…I'd wait till you fell asleep so I could cry myself to sleep… every day my resentment for you grew…every day, I got sadder and felt more numb. I couldn't breathe…I hated you…but most of all, I hated myself,' Ellie admits for the first time, weeping, looking over to Frank, taking a breath and wiping away tears, 'I'm so sorry—'

Frank yells, frightened at her. 'NO!' he shouts. Falling away, out of the bathroom, he shouts again, and picks up a lamp, throwing it across the room, which begins a fit of rage. All the hurt and pain and shit he's been carrying within him explodes and he trashes the cabin, shouting and throwing whatever objects he can lay his hands on until there's nothing more.

Heaving and exhausted, he slows, standing alone with his head hung low, slouched, surrounded by debris.

Ellie's voice drifts in from inside the bathroom, like smoke on the water, 'On the table next to the bed…there's a bible. Inside is the ticket.'

He looks over at the red Gideons bible.

'They let me keep it. What's left from the winnings is in a shoebox under the bed,' she murmurs. 'I know it's not why you came here. I guess I just...I dunno,' she trails off.

He glances down at the pistol in his hand, his Tweety Bird, taking in all she's been through—the grease, grime, and blood she's covered in. The battered yellow electrical tape around the grip: stained. He holds his head up, looking straight to the bathroom with clarity and a new sense of purpose.

Stepping inside, he saunters over to Ellie and places Tweety in her limp hand. 'You're gonna finish what you started,' forcing her grip around it.

'What?' she heaves, wrestling the pistol away. 'No.'

He flogs her with a backhand. Then flogs her again. Too weak to do anything more, she succumbs crying and grasps the pistol with both hands.

He stands, taking a few steps back. 'Here, I'll make it easier,' and throws his arms open wide against the wall. Glancing out the bathroom door as the early dawn sun hits his eyes, he winces, and at that moment, a bullet rips through his neck, just under his right ear. Blood skims across the wall behind him.

His pistol hits the ground with a thud.

He grasps at his neck—eyes wide and stunned. Immediately, two more shots ring out, following in succession, hitting him in the chest. A curtain of blood sprays the wall behind him and he falls backwards, slumping into the corner of the bathroom.

All becomes eerily quiet. Footsteps creek. O'Leary steps into the bathroom, one hand bandaged, and the other with his gun aimed. He walks over to Frank's slumped body, a grin curling his lips, and he leans in, whispering, 'Looks like I won the fucking lottery.'

He quickly turns, hearing Ellie moan as she shivers with shock in the bathtub. He glares through her, disgusted. Aiming, he fires without hesitation and the back of her head explodes, the bullet doing its work, painting the tiles behind her. He nods to himself and steps out.

Spotting the red Gideons bible, he curiously picks it up and flips it to the back. Inside is the blood-stained lottery ticket. He tosses it aside amongst the rubble, crouches alongside the bed and sees the shoebox. He rests his pistol on the bed and lowers himself, lying on his stomach, squirming to reach under the bed. Finally grasping the shoebox, he pulls himself out and stands. Opening it, he peers inside. There are several wads of cash made up mostly of hundred dollar notes with several loose fifties.

He smirks, chuffed. 'Must be over a hundred grand here—you fuckin' beauty!'

Light shifts and a shadow falls across him. He looks up. Standing silhouetted at the door is Candy. He drops the shoebox. As he quickly reaches for his pistol, several bullets violently tear holes deep into his chest, stopping him short. He collapses. His blue eyes roll back into his head. Candy walks in and stands over his body, kicking him to be sure he's dead. He doesn't stir. She collects the wads of cash from the floor, depositing them back into the shoebox. Looking over, she sees Frank slumped in the bathroom's corner.

Inside, she crouches beside him and with tearful fondness, kisses him on the cheek.

Sunrise shines on Candy as she leaves the cabin with the shoebox of cash, walking out into a new life.

The sun rises upon the lonely cabin with the rustle of tinsel and the chime of bells in the breeze and Frank wakes abruptly in a pool of blood, as if emerging from a nightmare. There is warmth but also a gripping fear of the unknown, akin to a child who's wet the bed. He stares vacantly at the ceiling corner. Tears well, trailing down his cheek. It isn't his entire life that flashes before his eyes, but the spiritual eye of his heart—a warm ray of the holiest of light blossoms through the fabric of reality in front of him. A woman in a white linen shirt slowly becomes visible, appearing like the angel Gabriel once did, sent from God before Mary with a message of hope. It's just like the stories about angels his mother used to tell him when he was a kid. He can't help but stare, transfixed, awestruck, unable to move, but unafraid.

The woman steps forward from the radiant aura—It's Angel. She smiles lovingly upon him and draws near.

Gently, she caresses his cheek, whispering, *'Not yet.'*

"It seems that where demons fail and monsters falter…angels may prevail."

— Alan Moore
Swamp Thing (Vol. 2) #27. DC COMICS.

EPILOGUE

I wake up slowly. My ears attune to the faint whir of a fan. My eyes hurt, and so does my body. The first thing I see is a ceiling fan spinning above me. I sit up. My joints are stiff and aching. I'm in a room that looks something like a cabin with raw timber walls. The parching heat and dry air are immediate and impossible to escape. I hear whispers and shushing of children.

To my right, outside a window, are three cheeky aboriginal children peeking in. Upon looking at them, they flee, giggling as if caught, knowing they shouldn't be there. From where I lay, there are clear blue skies and the vast, flat red land of a rural place. *Where the hell am I?* A round breakfast table with a tray of fresh fruit and a jug of water is at the end of the room. As I get to my feet, I notice that someone has bandaged and wrapped my chest with heavy dressing gauze. I walk stiffly to the table and pour a glass of water, drinking it all in one hit, then pour another.

I remember the panic of knowing I was going to die. The thoughts of darkness, of not knowing what would follow. Nothing, no life, never to exist again, not even being aware. Just... gone for all of eternity—that used to scare me more than the possibility of Hell.

A familiar feeling takes over, something from my youth—the warmth of the sun upon my bare chest accompanied by the sound of waves on the beach. I can't understand it and I have trouble rationalising or explaining how I survived it—out at the cabin that morning—and how I was able to breathe with two bullet holes in my chest. But there I was, standing along the bank of the lake outside cabin 10, watching it burn to the ground as the day woke up. The howl of emergency sirens in the distance. The thick black plumes of smoke. The cracking snaps and pops as the flames scream, reaching for the sun. The white disposable BIC smeared with blood in my hand and the presence of someone alongside me I couldn't see. I wasn't alone.

Darkness followed soon after, and again, my memory failed. There was no flash, no image, sound, or even something murky…perhaps I'm not meant to remember.

That sound again, the rustling of tinsel and the chime of bells in the breeze. I turn and behind me seated on the windowsill, smiling proudly with radiant beauty with the sun glowing behind her is my angel. *Hey Angel. Hey Angel.* She hops off and glides towards me, smiling. I touch her cheek and she touches mine. We look deeply into each other's eyes, our lips close and it occurs to me, that it's time to say goodbye—and she knows. That's why she's here. I ask her for one last kiss, one last time, just to know I'm not dreaming, just to know that it was all worth it. Just to know. I shut my eyes. We kiss. I open my eyes slowly. They don't hurt. She's gone.

There's an oak-encased pen next to the fruit tray. It has my name engraved on it. I sit down at the table. The old bloke's coat hangs off the back of the wooden chair. The journal Angel gifted me is in the left pocket—somehow, it has survived. I know the time's right, so I take the journal from the old bloke's coat. I have a story to tell, so I begin writing.

Some people are haunted by the past, whereas others are guided by it.

Acknowledgments.

Coffee (Magic).
Family and Friends, you know who you are.
But most of all, my angel Hannah.

Thank you for joining me on this journey through "Hey Angel." Your thoughts and feedback mean the world to me. If you have a moment, I would love to hear your review. It helps more readers discover this story!

amazon.com

goodreads.com

Music referenced...